Once and Future Lovers

a Collection of Short Fiction

Sheree L. Greer

Reviews

"There is no doubt in my mind the short fiction here will leave readers enthralled, charmed."

Claudia Moss, *If You Love Me, Come*

"The moment I finished reading *Once and Future Lovers*, I took a deep breath and then exhaled. It seems like ages since I've been this enthusiastic about a newly discovered writer... In each of these short stories she has crafted images that are simultaneously simple and profound. She has woven phrases that demand a second reading."

Renee Bess, author of *Between a Rock and a Soft Place*

"Greer writes with intention and the majority of the stories feel deeply personal. The stories are slathered in authentic, human experiences, whether good or bad. The author digs into her characters to unearth their desires and faults. For me, this is the stuff good short stories are made of."
Lauren Cherelle, editor at *Black Lesbian Press* and *Black Lesbian Literary Collective*

"Love. The four-letter word conjures so many images and thoughts and emotions that can be hard to express. Sheree L. Greer captures the sentiments beautifully in her short story collection, *Once and Future Lovers.* Her book highlights the simplest and most complicated forms of affection from the romantic to the familial... The narration of each story exudes genuine human interactions that are relatable to any sexuality, race or gender. Love can't be defined by those things, and Greer presents this knowledge in a splendid way."

Rena, reviewer at Sistahs on the Shelf

"I love for an author to take me there and to implant characters in my heart that I'll never forget. That's exactly what this book did for me. I was able to feel. A collection of unforgettable, well-written, diversified stories."

Trelani Michelle, author of Women Who Ain't Afraid to Curse When Communicating with God

"After reading this amazing debut, I once again believe in the power of words to move and inspire a human heart. Sheree Greer's fiction is alive on the page. It reaches up and grabs at your heart and won't let you go until long after you've read the last word. I believe in the power of fiction again because of this great collection. Do yourself a favor and begin to believe too."

Tony Bowers, author of On the Nine

Once and Future Lovers: Tenth Anniversary Edition

Write On Point || ISBN: 979-8-9874732-0-7

These are works of fiction. Any resemblance to locations, events, or actual persons, living or dead, is purely coincidental.

"Christmas is Sacred" originally appeared in *Windy City Times*.

"I Do All My Own Stunts" originally appeared in *Bike Shorts*.

"We Call Love Longed For" originally appeared in *Whimsicalit: an Unfolding Magazine* and *Badass Black Girl*

"The Liar" originally appeared in *Windy City Queer: Dispatches from the Third Coast*

"Dreaming Woman" and "The Beginning of Something" is excerpted from the novel-in-progress, *What Has Never Been Taught*

Cover design by Chastity Pascoe, Work With Seed Marketing & Design

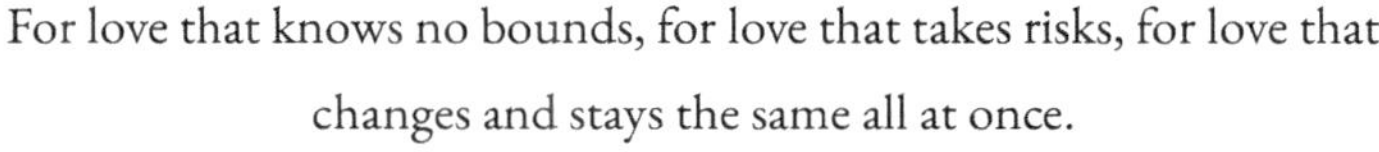

For love that knows no bounds, for love that takes risks, for love that
changes and stays the same all at once.

For Jasmine.

Stories

I Do All My Own Stunts	1
Dreaming Woman	6
Christmas is Sacred	18
S	21
The Beginning of Something	24
Commitment Phobia	47
The Liar	64
Baby Girl	82
We Call Love Longed For	87

I Do All My Own Stunts

1983

I used to ride Shadow, my black tricycle, with no hands. When I was four, I managed to stand up on the hard, black metallic seat while the bike sped towards the end of my block. I hit a bump, went flying over the handlebars and landed face-first on the concrete. The sting of my skinned knees, palms, and elbows, the blood rushing from my newly loosened teeth, and throbbing in my head should have taught me a lesson.

1991

I hated the pink and white, hand-me-down Huffy I got for my eleventh birthday. It had U-shaped handlebars, a scratched-up white frame, and a hideously soft, pink vinyl banana seat. I hated that the bike was pink and white. I hated that it had that long, ridiculous seat.

Nevertheless, I rode that Princess Pink Huffy like the BMX I wished it was. I rode with no hands. I jumped off curbs. I pedaled as fast as I could and leapt off that thing like it was on fire, sending it ghost-style up the alley until it slammed into a garage door or dumpster. It was a resilient piece of machinery. But one too many ghost-riders sent me to my doom.

One day, I rode full speed towards the bar of cement in the front of our parking space to pop a wheelie I could be proud of, catch some air that would make me gasp. I made it to the cement bar. I pulled up at the right moment. I screamed as the Huffy abandoned me in mid-air, diving forward as the handlebars and bike frame parted ways.

I landed on my back, blood from my lacerated tongue filling my mouth, and U-shaped handlebars still in my sweaty hands. The damage was ir-reparable, and I spent the rest of the summer with no bike at all.

1994

I have never gotten a brand-new bike. At fourteen, I was riding my father's blue Trek ten-speed. The bike was in fairly good shape and had I aspirations for winning the Tour de France, perhaps I would have appreciated the lightweight frame, the ram horn, drop handlebars, and the thin, 27-inch wheels a bit more. Still, I whipped through the streets of my neighborhood with my ten-speed, switching gears and winding my pedals backwards to make that rattling clicking sound. Riding that bike made me feel grown-up, made me feel fearless. At the time, I believed those feelings to be one in the same.

In a test to that sentiment, I walked into a neighborhood challenge brave and hellbent on success.

My sometimes friend, most times arch-nemesis Randy had a ramp. His father built it for him and would drag it out of the garage and into the center of the alley on the weekends. Everyone in the neighborhood talked about the ramp. Who could jump it and who couldn't; who was scared and who wasn't. I may not have been properly equipped, but I could surely make the jump and I most definitely wasn't scared. I decided to do it.

Randy and his crew of towheaded, lanky followers stood around waiting for me to bail. I did no such thing.

Pedaling, as fast as I could, knuckles stretch-yellow around the curl of the padded handlebars, I zoomed toward the shoddy looking ramp. I went up the curve, caught a split-second of air, and slammed into the concrete below. I didn't fall right away. I just stood. Paralyzed by pain.

My hand-me-down ten-speed was made in the grand tradition of gender-specificity. It was a men's bike. It was blue. It was fast. It had one of those heinous bars across the top of the frame. If I had had balls, I would've been injured into sterility. Having recently discovered myself, deftly learning how to press and rub myself into a guilty explosion of heat and stifled gasps, I worried about the damage that could have actually been done.

My clitoris, I thought, when and if it would stop stinging and aching, was most definitely broken. I finally fell over, grabbing my crotch and cursing through clenched teeth.

A week later, I started my period and though I knew better, I convinced myself I was dying.

2002

My girlfriend gave me a bike. It needed a little work, but it was the thought that counted. I had told her I wanted a bike, and she brought me one. Just like that. "It just needs a chain," Faida had said. A few months ago when we broke up, I told her I didn't want to. But we did. Just like that. "I just need a change," she said.

I would see her around the city, a bold contrast to everything around her. The city a blur of watercolor, and in all of Chicago, only she was clear to me: her body—modest breasts underneath a plain white t-shirt, no bra, hips that gave life to jeans made to hug them, and her face—skin bright and electric as copper wire, large eyes and wide mouth hungry for experience. I would look at her, then look away when she met my eyes. Faida wanted to be friends. I couldn't bear it. She would call me. I wouldn't answer. Her voice hurt my ears. My chest ached for the weight of her, the press of her face or her breasts against mine.

My favorite memory of her and me is the night we stayed up playing chess until just before dawn. Faida had knocked over the remaining chess pieces, all of them, our queens, our kings, our ambling pawns, her knight and last bishop, the one rook I was holding on to; I was losing but didn't care. Abandoning the game, we ran hand-in-hand the three blocks to Rainbow Beach. When we arrived, Faida wrapped her arms around me, resting her chin on my shoulder. We watched the sun rise on the rocky beach. The sun, a perfect disc of hopeful orange, pushed up from the horizon, changing the sky into a collection of paint strokes: chartreuse, fuchsia, turquoise, and periwinkle chasing away the midnight blues.

"Tell me some stories about you," she whispered. Her breath smelled like licorice.

I told her my bike stories.

She laughed at each one. "Good thing physical pain is temporary," she had said, kissing me just beneath my ear.

Every time I look at the white Trek mountain bike, still sitting in the hall, still needing a chain, my throat double-clutches and my mind begins to race. I remember everything about her: the dimple in her left cheek; the moon-shaped scar behind her right knee; her loud, head-turning laugh; the way she ate baby carrots straight out the bag; how she never washed her fruit and rolled her eyes at my threats that I wouldn't kiss her for the germs; her hands on me, under me, inside me; her tears and snot and slob drying shiny and stiff on my shirt when she fell asleep in my arms the day her grandfather died; the first time she told me she loved me—an unlined note-card left on my pillow, the words scrawled in silver crayon, all caps.

I struggle to switch gears. Riding the Trek through memory is rugged terrain. I hit one rock after another, blinded by the light of the rising sun. Old wounds long since healed begin to itch and sting. My hands, my mouth, my clit. I slam on the brakes and my heart screeches, sliding, the tread a bit worn. I go flying forward, weightless, free and happy for mere seconds, the imminent crash into reality already scraping my skin and breaking my bones.

Dreaming Woman

Daryan and Zaire had made a date for Saturday. She would pick Zaire up, and they'd go back to her place to watch *Raisin in the Sun*. When Saturday came, Zaire woke to the sound of her mother's heavy footsteps coming down the stairs. She knew, as she waited for her to appear out of the darkness of the basement, plans were about to change.

Robin sat on the end of her daughter's bed and told her she was going in for overtime. Sierra wasn't to be left alone with Mama Iris all day, especially since Mama Iris hadn't had the best week. She had been having nightmares about rats and increased incontinence, and lately, had taken to referencing Sierra as 'that girl.' It made for a trying time for all of them. Robin didn't say it explicitly, but Zaire suspected her mother used her own money to purchase Depends, handle doctor visit co-pays, and pay Sunshine Center bills for Mama Iris's care during the week.

"I really need to take advantage of this overtime, Zaire," Robin said, rubbing her wrists. She promised her daughter the next Saturday off. Zaire accepted, as if she had a choice, and walked with her mother upstairs and to the front door.

"You and Sierra are my angels," Robin said. "I appreciate you two so much, you know that?"

"Yes mama. We know." Zaire smiled and kissed her mother good bye.

On the weekends, taking care of Mama Iris seemed less hectic. The hustle of the weekday grind was brutal: getting up at dawn to get bathe and dress Mama Iris then bathe and dress herself, helping keep her little sister Sierra on time for her school bus, driving Mama Iris to the Sunshine Center for adult day care before dashing off to school herself, where she was perpetually late for homeroom and sometimes just made it in time for her first hour college math class. When Saturday and Sunday came, everything slowed down, the time Zaire and Mama Iris spent together shifted into an opportunity for Zaire's exhausted mind and restless heart to feel themselves.

Zaire stood over her grandmother's bed with her hands on her hips. The room reeked of piss, sharp and nearly lethal in its attack on her nostrils. "You ready?" She asked Mama Iris.

The older woman looked up at her granddaughter with greenish goo in the corner of her watery eyes. "I guess so." Mama Iris reached up to wrap her arms around Zaire's neck.

Zaire leaned over, the usual ache in her lower back greeting her quiet and familiar, a simmering heat that would gain momentum and rage through-out the night. She stretched her arms around and under her grandmother's body. She twisted her as she pulled, sitting Mama Iris upright until her legs dangled over the edge of the mattress.

And so it would begin, the arduous task of getting Mama Iris ready to greet the day.

It once seemed so overwhelming, so impossible. But what began as a slow, back-breaking, embarrassing, and sometimes nauseous duty had become routine, had gone from something Zaire had to do to something she simply did. Removing the wet nightgown, scrubbing her grandmother's smooth skin—flat breasts, pillow-soft belly, jiggling thighs and bottom—took on a familiarity equal to washing her own body.

"What you doin' today?" Mama Iris said. Zaire helped her stand up; her legs shook.

Almost trance-like, Zaire moved quickly through her grandmother's top half, dipping the wash cloth in a small, plastic basin filled with warm, soapy water, ringing out excess water, cleaning under arms and beneath breasts.

"Hanging with you," Zaire said with a wink before zipping out to the bathroom for fresh water to tackle Mama Iris's bottom half. She returned walking carefully, suds sloshing against the rim of the shallow wash bucket.

"Uh huh, until something better comes along." She held on to her granddaughter's shoulder with one hand and gripped the handle of her walker with the other.

Zaire removed her grandmother's sagging Depends. The nearly soaked, yellow and brown-stained cloth of the inside squished as she folded it best she could with one hand. She dropped the diaper to the floor with a thud while reaching over to the roll of paper-towels lying on the bed.

"Something better than hanging with you? No such thing." She wiped the shit and piss that dripped from the crack of Mama Iris's behind and threatened to drizzle down her thighs.

Mama Iris smacked her lips and turned one corner of her mouth up. Her body swayed a little as Zaire wiped.

"Well, at least you know." She smiled, the gold tooth in her dentures glinted. "Save me from havin' to tell you."

The two of them shared a laugh as Zaire reached over to retrieve the sudsy cloth from the plastic tub.

"You can't charm a charmer," Mama Iris said.

Shaking her head, Zaire couldn't help chuckling. Sometimes, Mama Iris had a way of smiling, flashing that gold tooth, and saying something so clever or funny, the chore became quality time; the inconvenience became intimacy.

Zaire squeezed water from the washcloth, worked up a lather with the soft, melting bar of Dial at the bottom of the basin, then washed her grandmother's most private parts; parts, that without almost without warning, go from simple anatomy—sexless, merely biological—to a mystery, a special secret to be revealed carefully, cautiously. Washing her grandmother, Zaire wonders if aging brings the body back again, from passionate to perfunctory; the intimate knowledge and varied experience disappearing or drying up, leaving only wispy gray hairs curling against themselves. Or, is Mama Iris's sex still alive—as animated and surprisingly quick as her smile is? Maybe along the very folds Zaire traces and dips into with a timid cloth, live fervent, provocative feelings she will keep hidden alongside those she cannot deny. Zaire thought of the secrets that lived within her. Deep inside the guarded darkness between her legs, Zaire kept a hushed account of her dreams.

She did her best to ignore her dreams, shamefully shutting them out of her everyday life, trying to forget them the second she woke up, forcing herself to consider some other thing, anything, everything—her boyfriend, her friends, her family, college applications, the new metal detectors to be installed at Adams, how many Kangols Daddy Arthur actually owned, the upcoming AP English exam, the new Mountain Dew flavor. She tried in vain to bury the sensations that greeted her each night when she closed her eyes.

The dreams, more and more vivid each time, started as a soft presence, a closeness warming behind her, a presence faceless and gentle. Then a feeling of breath against her neck that grew to a sensation of skin like silk at her back, fingers touching her with care, intention, lust.

Finally, the night fantasies asserted themselves fully: Daryan, standing behind Zaire, both of them naked. Zaire feels her friend's nipples grazing her shoulder blades as she inhales, and when she exhales, a sweet sigh escaping her throat, Zaire feels her breath, hot and urgent, against the back of her neck, compelling her to turn around. When she does, Daryan smiles a smile Zaire has given a thousand meanings—amusement, compassion, intrigue, invitation. Zaire smiles too, feeling weightless. Daryan places her warm, soft hands on Zaire's shoulders and her touch becomes the only thing that keeps her from floating away.

Zaire awakes to the sound of her own gasp, wrapped in the darkness of her bedroom. Sierra beside her, sleeping deeply; darkness is Zaire's only solitude, and it gives her a solace the slickness between her legs won't allow. She places her hand there, across the lips that thankfully never speak, to stifle feelings she prays are the kind that remain hidden and not the ones that cannot be denied. Afraid and trembling with shame, she clenches her eyes tight, praying herself back to sleep.

As Zaire bent down to gather the soiled paper-towels, mattress pads, and soaked Depends, the doorbell rang.

"Shit," she said under her breath, instantly remembering that she hadn't called Daryan regarding the change in plans. The bell rang again, a whimsical chime that ended on a jarring up-note because of a short in the wiring.

She scooped the garbage up. "Be right back," she said, helping her grandmother sit down on the bed.

"I ain't going anywhere," Mama Iris said with a shrug, tapping her fingers on the walker in front of her. Zaire grinned at her then cinched the trash in a plastic bag and dashed out of the room as the doorbell chimed one last time.

She pushed open the screen door and let Daryan step inside. Holding the plastic bag in her left arm, she gave her friend a one-armed embrace so catch and release it barely qualified as a hug.

"What's up? You ready?" Daryan asked, glancing at the other girl sideways. "You ain't ready." She stood just inside the door, looking comfortable and warm. She wore a hooded fleece pull-over the deep, fresh color of evergreens, a pair of faded jeans—white thermals poking out of two grape-fruit sized holes at the knees—and a puffy down vest, black with a white eagle over her breast. Though Daryan wore similar clothes to school every week, something about seeing Daryan on a weekend felt exciting, felt new.

Daryan put her hand on Zaire's shoulder and shook her head. "I knew you weren't going to be ready."

Zaire nodded, feeling like maybe she was blushing and wondering if there was any way to stop it.

"I'll explain in a minute. Have a seat."

Daryan squeezed Zaire's shoulder before going over to the couch to sit down.

"So, my mother ended up working today," Zaire said upon returning from taking out the small bag of trash. "I can't go anywhere until she gets off."

"Oh" Daryan shrugged. "Where's your sister?"

"Still sleeping," Zaire answered. "She's got to get her fifteen hours beauty rest." She laughed nervously.

"And Mama Iris?" Daryan looked around the living room.

"I'm not finished getting her dressed." Zaire smiled at her friend, moved at the way she referred to Mama Iris, lovingly though this was her first time meeting her. Zaire clasped her hands in front of her. She looked down and noticed a smudge of brownish-green shit near the base of her thumb. She scanned Daryan's arms and shoulders frantically, praying she hadn't gotten any on her.

"You can take off if you want. I'll call you later when my mama gets home," Zaire said.

She rarely had company over to the house anymore. She looked forward to opportunities to get out of the house, a place that, recently, possessed the trappings of work and duty rather than refuge and comfort.

Daryan had asked her friend once why she never invited her over, and Zaire shrugged through a real response. It seemed too hard to explain: the additional weight of having someone around while she struggled with her grandmother. She knew she'd feel Daryan's eyes on her, watching and wondering, shaking her head with the pity that most times bubbled beneath the surface of concern. Those feelings piled on top of her own feelings, which teetered consistently between sympathy and annoyance, responsibility and affection, would be too much to handle.

Daryan smiled, her full lips framing straight white teeth. "You sure? I can…"

"Yeah. I mean, it's fine. I'll call you and we'll do something later."

"Okay," Daryan said. She eyed her friend carefully, cutting her eyes in deep estimation.

Zaire met her stare and smiled to convince her everything was fine.

"Okay." She said again, nodding. "If you're cool, I'm cool." She stood up and stretched. "Guess I'll catch you later then. Maybe I'll drop the movie off later and we can watch it here." Her tone made the statement more like a question, giving Zaire a chance to change her mind.

"I'll call you," Zaire said. Holding herself against the cold blast of air, she held the screen door open. She shivered, the still chilly spring air seeping through the plastic taped over the screen, and watched Daryan walk up the cement path to her severely rusted Riviera.

"If you're cool, I'm cool." Zaire repeated to herself. It was almost laughable. Truth? Daryan was cool all on her own, evident even in her walk, long strides, certain steps.

Daryan glanced over her shoulder before walking around to the driver's side of her car. Zaire waved and she smiled, her trademark smile, the dream smile.

Mama Iris sat leaning slightly to the right. Her nipples at the ends of her drooping breasts kissed the bulge of her belly. She stretched her arm towards the shirt at the foot of the bed.

"Get that for me" she said.

Zaire handed her the shirt and watched her struggle with it; her left arm still drawn close to her body but fingers moving, grabbing towards the neck of the shirt. Zaire stood awkwardly. Helping too soon translated to a pity she tried to hide and loaded the air with a condescension that would suffocate them both. Yet, watching too long made her feel cruel, even sorrier for her grandmother, as she held back the assistance she knew the older woman needed but would never outwardly request. Zaire struggled for balance, but could never decide on how many seconds or minutes or breaths it took before respecting her grandmother's dignity became torturing her wavering sense of independence.

She took a deep breath then leaned in to help Mama Iris get the shirt over her head.

"No bra today?" she asked.

Mama Iris grinned. "Grab me one out that drawer."

"You don't have to wear one, you know." Zaire winked.

"I ain't fast like you," her grandmother said.

Laughing, Zaire fished a bra out of the drawer. She lifted her grandmother's soft breasts gently, cradling their heft in her palm. Old breasts in young hands, the gesture seemed symbolic of the future somehow, so she moved extra carefully, like Mama Iris was made of glass. Her arms limp at her side, almost non-existent, she was Venus crafted in crystal. Zaire slowly settled the older woman's breasts in the cups of the bra, and Mama Iris sighed as her granddaughter struggled to latch the tiny hooks in back.

When she finally got it, both grandmother and granddaughter sighed.

Zaire put the finishing touches on her grandmother, stretching her shirt over her head, pulling it down, and adjusting it. Helping Mama Iris stand on her walker, Zaire worked on a fresh Depends and helped her grandmother step into her pants.

"I got you," Zaire said, pulling the pants up. "Ready to eat?"

"Guess so," Mama Iris said.

Zaire liked asking her grandmother what she wanted, even when she knew the answer, even when there was no real choice and things would go the way they went: she would be washed and dressed then walked out to the living room where she'd watch television while Zaire fixed her brunch. At any rate, the questions created a sense of control, they deflated the bigness of the care-giving and care-receiving roles and made the routine more about trust and love and respect.

The roles would balloon again though, become oversized and awkward at the most unsuspecting of moments—when Zaire prepared her grandmother's food, softly denied her more dessert, or decided it was time for her to lie down for a while.

While Mama Iris ate her breakfast of Special K with sliced banana, toast, and instant coffee, Zaire cleaned her bedroom and went into the bathroom to wash out her gown.

Zaire filled the bathroom sink with hot water and poured blue laundry detergent on Mama Iris's gown. She swooshed the gown around, kneading the cloth like dough, squeezing it between her fingers as suds began to froth and swell. The knuckles of her tired hands ached in the hot water. Steam rose from the sink and the smell of piss, shit and spring fresh detergent filled her nostrils. She twisted the heavy, cotton night gown between her hands, rubbing the fabric against itself.

She watched her own hands, losing herself in their automatic motion. The second they had reached into the water, they knew what to do. Zaire didn't remember ever being taught how to wash clothes in the sink, how to scour a gown or pair of panties clean by hand. But somehow her hands knew, as if filled with some ancient wisdom, some innate skill passed down through generations and generations of women's hands: cleaning, rubbing, holding, and birthing.

Zaire scrubbed more vigorously. Water splashed up into her face and suds popped onto the mirror above the sink. She wondered what else women's hands knew, or rather, what else her hands knew. They weren't that adept at fastening bras, a fatty crescent of breast always winked at her from beneath Mama Iris's underwire whenever she helped her with hers. She had no problem getting the bra off, though. She could even unsnap the hook with one hand, using a thumb and forefinger. She didn't remember being taught how to do that either. She just did it one day, taking off her own bra then a few times unhooking her mother's when Robin's arms were so tired she could barely lift them. Maybe Zaire learned it in a previous life, saw it done once and remembered it.

She closed her eyes and pushed her hands deeper into the sink. The hot water swallowed her fingers and palms and wrists. The heat radiated from her hands to her forearms to her biceps, up and up her arms, triceps to shoulders, neck and head. She felt breath, fierce and sweet, at the nape of her neck. Zaire's mouth went dry. She looked down at her trembling hands in the water then at her reflection in the mirror.

Daryan's face entered the frame behind her. Her friend's skin the deep, warm brown of simmering molasses, carrying the sweetness of her almond-shaped eyes adorned with dark, heavy lashes, her slender, serious face opening with a smile. She shifted, her breasts grazing Zaire's back, rubbing against her tank top. She licked her lips and leaned forward, pressing her mouth against the round of Zaire's shoulder. She held it there, her mouth, held it steady and intentional, her full lips parted ever so slightly, making the kiss three parts deliberate pressure and one part delicate sucking.

Zaire closed her eyes, or were they closed already? Or maybe she opened them. Did it matter? She created the moment as she imagined it, the feeling of it confusing, alluring, like a memory. She seemed to both dream and remember the sensation of Daryan's lips on her skin. Can you remember something that never happened? The recollection, the fantasy, unwavering, Zaire recalled what to do, an instinctual wisdom guiding her hands out of the water and behind, reaching behind, finding Daryan's wrists and pulling her arms around her waist. Zaire, held from behind, her friend's mouth on her shoulder, tried in vain to steel herself against the trembling in her stomach. She collapsed against Daryan, her bones liquefying, melting from the heat of it all.

Steam filled the hot bathroom, and it seemed longer than before—a corridor almost, a hallway stretching for an entire city block, then longer and longer, knowing no limits. The double vanity became sink after sink, mirror after mirror, cabinet after cabinet, a row of overhead lights burning on and on, timeless and forever. There were no boundaries. Everything—the bathroom, the kiss, the feeling—eternal and infinite. Then, as Daryan lifted her lips from Zaire's shoulder, it all snapped back like a rubber band against her wrist. Reality stinging her skin in a short, tense, jolting instant.

A soft moan escaped Zaire's lips. The sound of her own voice startled her. Panting, she swallowed hard and looked around. Alone in the bathroom. Her face flushed, red and hot. She lifted her dripping hands from her thighs, leaving dark blue handprints on her jeans.

Reminded of her duty, Zaire's hands recalled their charge; she slipped them back into the water, rinsed the gown, and squeezed it over the bathtub, wincing and biting her lip. She threw it over the shower rod. She stood for a moment, watching water drip from the hem then took a deep breath, trying to clear her head of where her mind had gone, and how completely. It scared her.

Everything felt heavy. Zaire wanted things to be light and dry, so she could fold it and tuck it neatly away, push it to the back in the drawer of her mind, forget about it, lose it even. But her heart, her mind, her body, time, everything just seemed too heavy, too wet.

Christmas is Sacred

December 23, 2006 10:07 p.m.

It's a race. I will lose because Rayna never wears a bra. We squirm out of our sweaters. Then, tank tops fling over heads, belts rip through loops, jeans down hot thighs. We step out of them, arms stretched out for balance as we carefully wobbled ourselves free. Thongs slide from ass cracks, swing around ankles and get kicked into the air. I snap my bra hook with a single hand and peel it off my moist breasts.

"I want to fuck you" I say.

With Rayna against the wall, her legs on my shoulders and me on my knees, I lick and suck her until her thighs threaten to snap my neck.

"JESUS CHRIST!" she screams.

We collapse to the carpet in a heap of sweaty skin, aching muscles, and trembling arms and legs.

December 24, 2006 8:16 p.m.

Rayna and I lie on the floor naked in front of the couch. My heart bounces around in my chest like a pinball, clicking and ringing and giving me a thousand more plays.

"I gotta go to church tomorrow," Rayna says.

"Okay." I lick red wine off her skin like blood from an invisible wound.

"You gon' come?" She stretches. "I mean, it is Christmas."

"I don't really do the whole Christian thing," I say, trying not to sound irritated. When I came out to my mother two years ago, she said, "I'll pray for you." Last Thanksgiving, my aunt whispered "Abomination unto the Lord," when she thought I was out of ear shot. I don't tell Rayna any of this.

"You know," Rayna begins, rolling on top of me. Pressing her face into my neck, kissing me then sliding down. She stops at my breasts. My nipple is her microphone. "I still believe Jesus saves."

I don't mean to, but I giggle.

Rayna rolls her eyes, shakes her head, and goes down on me. I call out to God when I cum.

December 25, 2006 2:45 a.m. Christmas Day

I watch Rayna sleep.

Beads of water on her shoulder or the musky salt between her breasts—I want it. The crispy cool of her still bath-damp pubic hair or the tang of her marinating against Victoria Secret cotton all day—I want it. Sometimes I fear I'm but a caricature of desire. I am a tongue wearing glasses with enormous hands. I am taste and touch, and perhaps nothing more. I'm always broke. My mattress is on the floor in my bedroom. My stereo is piece of shit. I drink too much. I'm slow to anger but filled with rage. I am a struggling writer and struggling writers are mostly always poor and temperamental, difficult and dramatic. She is too good for me. When will she figure it out and leave me?

"What's wrong, baby?" Rayna says in her sleep. She takes me in her arms. I am wrapped in sweetness, in darkness, in something that could be love.

"Nothing," I say. I kiss Rayna's chin. I think about what she said, "I still believe Jesus saves." I really don't give a damn. I believe in her. 'That's fine' I should have said. Instead, I laughed. I laughed.

Rayna kisses my forehead and I thank God for her, for the night, for everything.

S

The way her fingers fidgeted, drumming against her thighs, betrayed the smile and steady gaze she gave me when I looked up at her. The candles flickered against the sweating, sky blue tiles of the bathroom. An aura of gentle orange whispered around the curves of her face. Her hair, a collection of two-strand twists that drew up against the humidity of the steaming bath, crowned her shadow, which rose tall and majestic on the ceiling. I still hadn't gotten used to her beauty. She inhaled deeply. She made fists with her hands before extending her fingers and returning them to the rhythmic drumming along the rounds of her thighs. I smiled at her. I had never seen her nervous before.

"Just be still," I whispered. I reached up and grabbed the small bar of cucumber-mint soap from the edge of the sink then worked it into the curly triangle of hair between her legs until it lathered.

She laughed. "Are you sure you know what you're doing?" she said, looking down at me.

"Yeah," I said. I squinted at my canvas then looked up into her face.

She raised an eyebrow, and though she didn't say anything more, her eyes spoke to me—no, they sang to me. They always did. Different songs at different times. Anita Baker, Maxwell, Marvin Gaye. That night, as the cool freshness of mint mingled with the warm, sweet musk of her natural scent, her eyes sang Minnie Ripperton. I nodded, hearing it, and hummed the chorus to "Inside My Love." I placed the soap back in the dish. I rinsed my hand in the bath water. I slid my hand around her ankles, my fingers dancing around the top of her foot, tapping her toes like piano keys. I pulled the stopper from the drain. The gurgle upset the quiet.

"You ready?" I asked. She nodded. I picked up the razor that lay on the small table next to the tub. She shifted. I pushed myself up a little higher on my knees and kissed the soft round of her paunch, a bead of water dancing out of her belly button as I pressed my mouth there. She sighed and rubbed her own thighs, her nails a flash of fluorescent pink and yellow.

I shaved slowly, soap and hair surrendering to the blade as I shaped the slopes and lines of my first initial. She didn't move. Her breath slow and deliberate, her soft sighs tightening my belly. I started singing the first verse as I got to work. Certainly more than a little off-key and slower than the actual tempo, I sang about spirits meeting and greeting, about being one separately then being one together. I hushed myself to focus, leaning in and biting my lip in concentration. The inner curves proved to be the hardest, moving the sharp, flat blade just right, pressing the straight edge at the perfect angle, negotiating the twists and turns.

I glanced up at her when I was done. She raised her eyebrows. I smiled. I cupped lukewarm water from around her ankles, the water nearly gone, and rinsed the dripping soap from my design. Sure, a little crude, but there it was.

An 'S.'

I leaned back and looked at it with one eye then the other.

"How does it look?" she asked. She held her head straight forward, her eyes closed tight as if afraid to look down.

I nodded, considering my design. I thought of the Minnie Ripperton album cover. Strange, recalling the image in that moment, or maybe not. Minnie Ripperton, topless in demin overalls, holding a melting ice cream cone. The playfulness and absurdity, the beauty and simplicity. The possibility.

The promise.

Everything in that moment, the heat of the bathroom, the dance of our shadows in the candlelight, the echoing drip of water from the spout, and the love between us, the playful, absurd, beautiful, simple, possibility that was us, felt like a promise.

"What?" she asked. "It's fucked up? It's fucked up ain't it?" She put her hands on her hips. "I don't want to look, she said shaking her head. She sighed and relented. She pulled up at her belly, lifting the weight of it, preparing to lean forward, stretching her neck forward with a sigh. "Say something," she said. "Get a mirror or something. I gotta see this thing. It's probably fucked up." She released her belly and laughed. "I bet it's all fucked up."

"It's not fucked up," I said. I smiled up at her. "It looks good." I said it quick, without spaces so it came out like one word. Like "yes." I leaned forward, smoothed the remaining hair down, and reared back once more to consider the design as a whole. She spread her legs and looked down at me. I glanced up, hoping to reassure her, wanting to tell her that nothing about us would ever be fucked up.

"It's perfect," I said.

She smiled. I smiled. I sat back and took in my work once again. The more I stared at it, the more it looked like a five.

I didn't care. And she didn't care either. It'd be mostly grown over in two weeks and gone within three. Not me though. Not us.

The Beginning of Something

Summer 1953

Arthur Turner

I know rocks and Earth. Hell, every day of my life till I was bout eleven and started chasin' after gals, I was damn near covered in dust and dirt. When I was a boy, I collected rocks, just jammed 'em in the pockets of my overalls. No particular reason I suppose. I just liked the hardness of them. The strength. I found out that the whole world, the Earth itself, ain't nothing but one big rock. I learned that from Mr. Simmons. The Simmons was some people my mama used to clean for down in Arkansas. Mr. Simmons was a historian. He had all kinds of pictures and books and curled up maps jammed in his office. What I liked most in his office though was the rocks. A whole case of rocks. Rocks sittin' up on shelves between and in front of the books. Some rounded and smooth. Some ragged and sharp. All of them dusty and old. I knew then that rocks ain't nothin' but history. The way they form land, the way they bury and preserve things, how they record the movement of water, all that is history. I made that connection early.

I used to go with my mama some days and Mr. Simmons would show me books and things in his study. This one day, he showed me this book with God's Finger in it. It's a rock formation out in the Canary Islands off the coast of Africa. I looked at God's Finger and at first, all I saw was a rock, a rock with a long tip on it. But Mr. Simmons told me how the people of the Canary Islands believed the rock was formed the way it was to tell them somethin', to make a point about who was supreme and who was responsible for not only all the rock formations in the world, not just all the water and the air, but who was the creator of everything.

That afternoon, Mr. Simmons told me about archaeology and the study of culture and civilizations all from rocks and artifacts people leave behind. I decided that afternoon that I wanted to be an archaeologist. He said he had wanted to be an archaeologist. When I asked him why he wasn't, he turned red and didn't want to talk about it. I figured if a white man couldn't be whatever he wanted what kinda chance did I have to be what I wanted.

I bounced around a bit in Arkansas doing yard work and after my mama died I hopped in a truck wit' my cousin Gooney and we drove nonstop up north, me cross-eyed from a jug of whiskey and him slit-eyed off reefer.

When I got up here, I got a job pouring cement for the city. Wasn't but a few of us in construction back then, at least not in city landscapin' and cement work. I liked the work because it took precision and skill to lay a sidewalk or pave a street. Had to be even and careful not to overfill or leave bumps, ridges, or protrusions and the like. I had a skill for it right off. Gooney got him one of them factory jobs. He worked at A.O. Smith. He had mostly worked as a mechanic down in Arkansas so it was a good fit. We both had good jobs, him at one of the big-time factories and me workin' for the city. We rented us a house over on Walnut, the upstairs of a duplex where two old ladies lived downstairs. Don't know if they was sisters or bull-daggers. Didn't really care, I suppose.

City life was decent. Me and Gooney worked hard and went out almost every weekend. We went to this place called Jimmy Cat's. The owner was a fat nigga with a face so shiny you could see your reflection in his big round cheeks. Fella had a gap between his two front teeth big enough to slide a pack of Lucky Strikes through.

Me and Gooney would meet in that joint on a payday and blow almost a whole check on whiskey and smokes. He was always slidin' his skinny ass right under a woman where she sat. He'd light her cigarette, buy her a drink, and have his hand on her ass before she even knew his name. He'd brag to me, make sure he made eye contact with me, and wink while noddin' in my direction. Like I gave a goddamn what bucktooth, cockeyed woman he done got to go out back with him. Except this one night. This one night I did give a goddamn.

I had been waitin' in Jimmy Cat's for about a half hour one Friday, cement still crusted on my steel-toes and my work vest dusty and hanging off my shoulders.

I was sittin' at the bar waitin' for Gooney but tryin' to look like I wasn't waitin' for him. I sat sippin' on my second E&J and finishin' up a third cigarette when a lady with her wig on crooked started makin' eyes at me and rubbin' the rim of her empty glass. I knew all about that hypnotic rim-rubbin' business. Thinkin' she gone pull a nigga in with the ultra-sonic squeal of her finger tracin' the rim of that glass, hypnotizin' a nigga to buy her drinks all night then end up buyin' her groceries befo' the end of the week. Shit, that's Gooney's pitfall, not mine. And maybe that makes me mean or hard. Shit, most people called me mean. I figure it's on account of me sayin' what's on my mind and lookin' people in the eye without flinchin.' Some other people probably said it cause I ain't the most attractive nigga you ever seen. But I ain't never gave a fuck about being so-called 'good-lookin'.' Anyway, only thing that gotta look good for a woman to give you some kissin' and squeezin' is your paycheck.

Anyhow, I got up to take a piss and as I walked past the side door, I saw Gooney's knotty head, A.O. Smith cap pushed back far from his face, right under a flickerin' Old Style sign. He shifted around the pole. I couldn't make out who he was talkin' to but I could see that nigga had the simplest smile I'd ever seen. He was leanin' back on his heels, hands behind his back like some kind of church usher. I forgot about goin' to piss and went out the side door.

There was a narrow walkway that led to dumpsters long side Jimmy Cat's make-shift parking lot. It was really just a slab of concrete riddled with broken glass and cigarette butts. Beside the overflowin' dumpsters there was a group of niggas all huddled together. They was passin' around a single cigarette between the four of them like a joint, hats smashed on they heads and hunchin' over like they was duckin' under a low ceiling. A siren flared up in the distance and the group of men shuffled a bit before breakin' up and dippin' round a corner. I continued up the walkway to where Gooney stood.

"Gooney, nigga, I been waitin' for yo' ass all night." I said.

He looked at me then at the ground. I followed his eyes from the dirty sidewalk to the light post. Against it, stood a woman so beautiful I bout lost my breath. She was lean but thick in certain places, the right places. Hips round and beckonin', breasts ready to bust out of her flowered dress, a small waist made for grabbin', and though the hem of her dress went past her knees, shit, you could tell by the length and shape of her calves that those legs was somethin' to slap your mama about. She stood with a hand on her hip and her other hand tappin' the ash off a cigar. Her skin was bout as light as the inside of an almond and her eyes, shit, her eyes was gray. Real gray like rain clouds buildin' just before it's bout to storm.

"This here my cousin Arthur," Gooney said. He was usin' this voice I ain't never heard before. It was light and quick. His voice was usually slow and thick like billows of reefer smoke tumblin' out his thin black lips. That nigga was nervous. "And Arthur, this... this here Christine."

"Pleasure," I said with a nod.

"Pleasure's all mine, Arthur." Christine took a puff of her cigar. She didn't blow out the smoke, she just parted her lips and curled her tongue up to the roof of her mouth and let the smoke roll out. The deep gray smoke, nearly the same color of her eyes, wafted up in front of her face.

The time that passed after those introductions felt like it was moving in slow motion. And it wasn't until I felt Gooney's sharp, bony elbow in my ribs that I realized I'd been starin'. I jumped and Christine laughed and caught her bottom lip between her teeth.

"Uh, sorry man, but uh, me and Christine was just talkin' and talkin' and I was tryin' to get her to come in for a drink." Gooney's lips was flappin' a mile a minute. I never knew he could even think that fast. "But she ain't really want to go inside, she said she wanted to stay out here and enjoy the fresh air. So I says I was gonna stand out here with her for a spell, you know keep her company and maybe have some fresh air for myself."

"Fresh air?" I chuckled. "Ain't nothin' fresh about the air or anythin' else around here." I looked over at the dumpsters and the oil-stained concrete slab. "Smell like piss, sweat and motor oil out here." I slid a Pall Mall between my lips and stuffed my hands in my pockets to feel around for my lighter. Came up with nothin'. I musta left it at the bar. I shot a quick glance at Christine.

Christine stubbed her cigar on the cement light post and threw the short, smashed left-over chunk into the street.

"You got a light?" The cigarette shook in the corner of my mouth as I spoke.

"Nope." Christine looked into my eyes and smirked. She had a purse slung over her shoulder crossways, the way they tell women to wear their purse for a nigga can't come up beside you real quick and snatch it from up under your armpit.

I knew she had a light in her purse. Ain't nobody ever smoked a cigar that ain't have their own matches or lighter or somethin'. Shit, she ain't want to give me no light, she ain't have to give me one.

"I'm bout to go back inside," I said.

"All right then, Arthur." Gooney took a half a step toward Christine then stopped. "I'mma stay out here then. You know, man, just keep Christine here company and all. I'mma be in there soon though, man, buy me a drink and…"

"I want to go inside," Christine said. Her voice was low and gritty. She stepped away from the light post and walked right between Gooney and me. She smelled like tobacco and smolderin' wood, but sweet too—like someone was cookin' maple syrup. She waited for Gooney to open the door for her, and we both followed her inside the bar.

Two hours had passed before I knew it. Christine ain't talk about herself much. She mostly let Gooney talk. We both did. Gooney was a good storyteller, goin' on and on about back home, talkin' shit about up north niggas and down home niggas in the same breath. Christine smiled and laughed but seemed distracted all the while, lookin' around the bar and watchin' the door like she expected the police to bust it down any minute. When Gooney slammed some money on the bar and said he was 'bout to go piss, I asked Christine why kept watchin' the door.

"I just like to know who coming and going," she said, then sipped her beer real slow.

"Look to me like you worried about somethin'."

"No. Just like to know who coming and going." She glanced at the door again.

I gave her the side eye and leaned back on the bar. We sat in silence for a spell, her lookin' at the door and all the place, me lookin' at her. Seemed like another hour passed time but I reckon it wasn't but ten or fifteen minutes. I sighed and pushed myself up from the edge of the bar.

"I'm bout to check on Gooney," I said. Christine nodded and finished her beer.

I went the pool table and saw Gooney slumped over on a stool near the back door. I shook him awake and that nigga just snorted and said somethin' about not wantin' to work today. I left him there and went back to the bar to tell Christine I needed to take Gooney home.

"Can you take me home, too?" Christine asked.

"Yeah," I said. "Meet me by my truck. It's blue. Right out front."

I collected Gooney and walked him to the truck. I pushed his narrow ass in the back of the cab then helped Christine into the passenger seat. She told me how to get to her house. It wasn't that far from the bar at all. She had me pull into the alley and drop her off in front of a dingy white and green garage.

"You gone be all right?" I asked. I thought about the way she was watchin' the door.

Christine smiled. Her gray eyes went softer and kinder than they been all night. "You're sweet, Arthur." She leaned over and kissed my cheek before she hopped out the truck and walked into the darkness between the garage and the bushes that lead to the back of the house.

After that night, I took to visitin' Christine at the garage. Most times I came to see her, she would look at me sideways while puffin' a pipe filled with reefer and Big Chief tobacco. The garage was behind the house where Christine and her younger sisters, Beulah and Little Iris, lived. Her father lived in the small, wooden house too, but I had yet to make his acquaintance and hoped I never would. Christine didn't talk about him, so I didn't bring him up.

The garage was large, anyhow, could easily fit two cars, with one door that lifted up into the rafters and a door around the side. It was painted white with green trim to match the house, every inch of that shit peeling. On them hot summer days, they kept the big door open, rolled all the way up or at least part-ways so you could duck in and out. A little furniture was scattered around with the other garage shit, shovels, rakes, and a rusted lawnmower.

It wasn't shit, but that's where we would hang—me, Christine, Beulah, and Gooney, who had forgiven me quick once he met Beulah.

Beulah and Christine shared some features, like you could tell they was sisters. But Beulah's eyes was big and brown. She was a little wider at the backside too and was a hell of a lot nicer. Shit, I didn't know what I had gotten myself into with Christine. Since that night we met, her kissin' me all soft on my cheek and callin' me "sweet," I hadn't even gotten a whiff of that thing if you know what I mean. It was like she clammed up or somethin'. She ain't let me touch her, and I couldn't remember the last time we had been alone.

In that garage, when Christine got in that ole rusty old chair, you could forget it. She'd be there frownin' at me and askin' me questions. All kinds of questions like do I have any bastard children runnin' around down south or how often I talk to my mother. I told her my mother was dead and she gave me the softest look I'd ever gotten from her. When I told her I walked out on the funeral, that look got sucked up so fast it was like it never really happened. Her dark gray eyes rolled like a storm and went all tight, just dark slits condemnin' me to hell.

Most times it was like she ain't even want me there, but she would ask about me every now and again if I ain't show up for a while. But then one day, I went to drop Gooney off, didn't plan on staying at all. It was pay day and wasn't no sense in settin' there wasting good drinkin' hours being judged by Christine when I could be settin' back tapping my foot to some blues.

So I dropped Gooney off and nodded at Christine.

"Where you off to in such a hurry?" She asked me through her pipe smoke.

"I gotta go home and get some shut eye. Gotta big job early in the morning, pays double since it's Saturday."

"Oh really."

"Yeah. Gonna make some long money tomorrow."

"Well, you ain't gotta leave right this second do you?" Christine asked. She patted the chair next to her.

Little Iris, Christine and Beulah's younger sister, came bustin' into the garage like the police. Everybody stopped. Me and Gooney tensed up—on account of always wonderin' when they daddy would come crashin' in with a shotgun and shovel. When we saw it was just her, we set back.

"What you want?" Beulah said.

"Nothing." Iris said. "I can't see how y'all just sit in here like this. It's hot. It stank. And y'all look bored."

"What's it to you?" Beulah said. "What we supposed to be doing? Playing jacks or something? It's grown folk business going on in here."

Gooney and Beulah busted up. Christine shook her head. I ain't say nothin' just kept an eye on Iris, wonderin' what she was gon' say next. Ain't never really watched her before. I knew she was fresh out of high school. Christine had said watching her graduate was one of the best days she'd had in a long time. She had big hopes for Iris, that Iris was special and could do anything she wanted. She was a firecracker, that much was sure. Pretty, yeah, all them Grady girls was pretty, but she had somethin' else. She wasn't all guarded and tough like Christine, but she wasn't all hammin' it up and sittin' ready like Beulah either.

"Beulah, baby," Iris got a twist in her neck. I knew something slick was coming. "I ain't played jacks in quite a while. Matter fact, the only games I been playing lately is the one your last boyfriend taught me."

Beulah smacked her lips and said, "Look here you little wretch, watch your mouth before—..."

"Wretch? Who you calling—..."

"Both of y'all just shut up," Christine said. "We got company."

"Company? I ain't really no company am I, Beulah baby?" Gooney rubbed Beulah's thigh. "I'm thinkin' 'bout moving in."

Everybody laughed but Christine. She looked at that nigga like he had two heads. Beulah just smiled and rubbed his bony ass knee. She didn't know what she was gettin' herself into with Gooney. That nigga was my ace, but he was simple and I believed he had left at least one nappy headed youngin' down there in Arkansas. Not sure if it was true, but he was sure in a hurry to get outta dodge. He kept a job sure, but wasn't no real provider.

Nigga made just as much or maybe even more money than me and still asked me to float him some bread sometimes. I shook my head hoping Beulah wasn't too serious about hitchin' her wagon to that horse-head fool.

"Well, I was just leaving anyhow." I stood up to go. Christine grabbed my leg. She done touched me twice in one afternoon. Something was up, hell if I knew what it was.

"You ain't got to leave." Little Iris said. "I'll go. It's too hot in here anyway." She dug around in her purse, dropped a handkerchief, picked it up all slow motion where I couldn't help but check out her pumped up bosom and strong thighs, then left the garage.

I sat back down and pushed my cap back on my head. I looked at Christine, curious of why she was so eager for me to stay all of sudden but didn't ask her nothin'. Beulah and Gooney went back to talkin' and Christine lit up her pipe. She stared at the door, puffin', always puffin', and not saying a goddamn word.

"I'm outta here." I stood up and paused for Christine to stop me. When she didn't, I left the garage.

Iris Grady

I had watched Arthur each time he came over with Gooney to see Beulah and Christine. I would show my face in the garage, but they'd shoo me away telling me I was too young, and I would just laugh and laugh. Too young for what is what I wanted to know.

At eighteen, I had already had more boyfriends than Christine, who was twenty-six, and Beulah, who had turned twenty-one a few weeks ago. Of course, my boyfriends were all young boys that didn't have a whole lot of experience or things going for them, but at least I was out meeting people, trying to get a life started. I refused to stay in that house, sharing the same room and bed I'd been sharing since before I could remember. I needed a life. We all did.

I craved an exciting life more than anything, more than anyone else I've ever met. I guess the only one that came close was Beulah. For her birthday, we had gone to a house-party around the corner. It was just a bunch of chumps drinking and smoking reefer in a finished basement—meaning it had a couch, card table with folding chairs, and a no roaches. The records were spinning all the hits and it only cost a dime to get in. We both met some knotty-headed fools, but it didn't amount to much. The important thing was that we was out, beyond the walls of the house, far away from the garage.

I didn't know what Christine thought about having a life, having a future. She never spoke of anything farther ahead than the next day and even that was a stretch. She seemed utterly contented to sit in that garage, smoking and drinking and waiting on me or Beulah to come in with some story about what was going on out in the world.

People noticed, of course, living all on top of one another like all colored people did in this neighborhood. I heard them. They called her queer or crazy or both. I even been asked outright, 'Why a beautiful girl like Christine keep herself all locked up in that garage?' Sure, she went out to the grocery store and stopped in the bank to deposit Daddy's social security checks, but she ain't really go out-out.

They called Christine odd and said it was unnatural for a young woman to stay at home with a shut-in father while her two sisters were out in the world. I would take up for her. Maybe the way Christine was just the way she was, and she'd go out and live her life when she was good and ready.

I thought she was good and ready when she brought Gooney and Arthur over. Shoot, I had to see if the sky was falling when I found out Christine had gone out at night and met Arthur and Gooney all on her own. First time I had ever heard of her going out at night, going to a bar, or meeting some men for that matter. I figured maybe she was tired of people talking, but even that puzzled me because she ain't never been shook by what people said about her.

I didn't know what to think. Christine brought Arthur and Gooney into the garage like she was bringing home groceries. She seemed bored the second they started hanging out regularly. It was written all over her face every time I stopped in there. Beulah was glad, though. She was too excited to have Gooney in her face. She always struck me as the type to get hitched up with someone or another and make it work from there.

I wasn't interested in no set-ups. I wanted to travel the world. The catch is, you can't really travel the world alone and I've never heard of a woman—especially a colored woman—going all over the world by herself anyhow. So, I knew I would have to meet a man with a good job, money, with his own desire to travel and see new places. Or maybe just a man with some money and experience. Either way, we'd both be fed up with this no-count town dressed up as a city and hit the road, maybe even cross the ocean.

In my mind, I'd know him when I saw him and we'd lock eyes and the rest would be history. I'd send my sisters postcards with silhouettes of giraffes against a glowing pink and orange sunset kissing tall golden grasses. I'd write something sweet and sophisticated on it like, 'The Motherland is beautiful... best wishes to your home from the home of all civilization!'

Only problem was the boys I'd been taking up with only wanted one thing. I'd string them along as long as I could, get them to buy me things, spend a few dollars on a bottle of gin, and when they got to getting too touchy-feely, I'd usually dump them. Don't get me wrong, I ain't no virgin and don't mean to make it seem so, but I need it to be clear I was in the market for more than a roll in the hay.

My plan was this: I'd meet a man that knew how to save money, wasn't afraid of working, and was both practical and magical. What I mean by magical? I mean a man that can see that this world, this life, is what you make it. A man who knows that sitting around in a garage smoking and drinking wasn't all there was to life. A man who knew of other worlds and wanted to see them. That's what I thought I found in Arthur.

I went into the garage one night after hanging with a few friends of mine at the park. I was feeling pretty good. Christine, Beulah, Arthur, and that simple-looking Gooney were all sitting around, looking as unaffected by the world as they always did. Gooney was leaning over whispering to Beulah with his long fingers drumming her knee. As usual, Christine was smoking and ignoring Arthur. They all jumped when I pushed open the door, then they all paused for a split second and went on with their sad little visit.

I kept looking at Arthur, checking him out, trying to make eye contact. He looked at me a few times. The only thing I could read on his face was that he was ready to go. I wanted to sit with them, to be near Arthur and see if my hunch was right—that Christine didn't really want him. As soon as I tried to make conversation, Beulah and I got into it. We were always getting into it over nothing. Hot-to-trot heifer always think I'm trying to take her man. Gooney? Please. Her song and dance spoiled the whole mood and Arthur was going to leave. I knew it was just me being there that had ruffled Beulah's feathers so I figured I'd be the one to leave.

But before I left and just to irritate Beulah, and maybe to tempt Arthur a little bit, I dug around in my purse for my cigarettes. My handkerchief fell to the floor. I bent down and lowered myself slowly. I took hold of the handkerchief right at the corner with the embroidered robin. I hunched my shoulders forward so the fullness of my breast rose up, nearly spilling out the front of my dress. Gooney and Arthur's eyes were buried so deep in my bosom, I could feel their eyelashes tickling my nipples. Ha! I snatched the handkerchief up and threw a smile at everyone before I switched my hips out the door.

I sat on a wooden crate around the side of the house, smoking and waiting for Arthur to come from the garage. When I saw him coming up the path, I crossed my legs and bounced my sandal off my foot. He came up the walk-way overrun with weeds and dandelions and had to stop in front of me, my foot blocking his way.

I took a pull of my Virginia Slim and acted like I didn't realize he couldn't get pass my foot without me moving it.

"Excuse me," Arthur said.

I didn't move.

"You gon' move yo' foot so I can get by?"

"You real country." I smiled at him. "Where you from, Arthur?"

His wide mouth curled on one end. He took a cigarette out his pack and slid it between his full lips. He looked at me, white cigarette dangling from the corner of his mouth.

"I ain't from here, that's fo' sure."

"Well, I know that." I stopped bouncing my foot. "Why else would I ask?"

Arthur bucked his eyes at me then nodded. He looked like maybe he wanted to smile but wasn't sure if he should. We stared at each other for a minute, sort of sizing each other I suppose. The dim light outside the side-door of the house bounced off his bald head, making a sort of spotlight on his hard face. His eyes were dark brown and playful, but his short nose and hard lined, pock-marked cheeks made him look intense and serious. He was older, that much was clear. With his weathered face and hard jaw, I guessed he was at least five years older than Christine.

"Guess you ain't in the mood for conversation." I moved my foot so he could pass. He shifted the cigarette in his lips and dug around in the pockets of his overalls. I held out my cigarette to him and he smiled. He took it from me, and our fingers touched for the slightest moment. It was something electric in it and I felt my face go hot. He wasn't that cute, but he had this way about him, like he had been places, seen things.

When he lit his cigarette with mine, the place where they met glowed red. He handed my cigarette back to me, took a long drag of his own and blew the smoke into the air over his head. Arthur watched the smoke coil on itself and float out of sight. I watched him.

He looked to me like he dreamt of far-away places and had even been to a few. The attraction was that he was older than me, had experienced more than me, and I could tell by the boredom settled on his face in the garage that he wanted more. I wanted more, too. I wanted him.

As if reading my thoughts, Arthur cleared his throat and kicked at a rock on the ground.

"You know I'm wit' yo' sister." He took a deep drag of his Pall Mall.

"Would she say that? That you're with her?" I said. I smoked the last of my cigarette and stubbed it out on the ground, giving us both a minute to think of Christine, to think of the garage.

Arthur looked down at his cigarette as if it could give him the answer. He licked his lips and smirked at me. "I don't know what she'd say." He chuckled and took a pull of his cigarette.

The signs were easy to see, and he didn't seem like the type to ignore what was plain as day. You could tell by the way Christine blew out her smoke when Arthur was around—all slow and careful, puffing her lips a little to make circles then watching them thin out and disappear—that she wasn't really interested. Not to mention, they never went anywhere. Christine would probably live in the garage if Wisconsin winters didn't get so cold. She'd sit right in that rusted chair and smoke that pipe until trumpets sounded.

"That's something," I said with a smile.

Arthur looked at me like I had asked a question. He sagged a little on his bow-legs and shrugged.

He took a cap out of his back pocket and slapped it on his head. "I should get going."

"Good night, then." I stood up.

"Good night," Arthur said. I watched him walk away.

That night, before we went to sleep—Buelah, Christine and me—I announced into the darkness that I liked Arthur. Beulah sucked her teeth and sighed. Christine yawned. Silence filled our small, crowded room.

"Have him," Christine said in a low, husky voice. She didn't even seem to think about it.

I had thought she'd say that but wanted to be sure. Beulah was silent, but I felt her shake her head. I'm sure she would talk mess later and other people might have something to say, but I decided there in bed, toe-to-head with Beulah, that I didn't care. I turned my face towards the wall and smiled, Beulah's sour-smelling stocking feet already digging into my back.

The Beginning of Something

Indian Summer kept autumn at bay. Arthur drove Iris far from the city proper. They rode in silence, listening to the radio, mostly blues and jazz. Iris looked out the window and Arthur mostly kept his eyes on the road, except for the few times he stole a glance at Iris's profile.

They parked off some side road. Arthur had driven them northwest off I-94 to a small fishing hole he and Gooney frequented. He wanted to be alone with Iris, completely alone, just her and him and the stars. No, the entire sky. For Arthur it represented peace and a space to just be. For Iris it was infinite possibility.

Arthur killed the engine and climbed out of the cab of his light blue Ford. He walked around to open the door for Iris and led her by the hand to the back of the truck. Helping her step up onto the bed, Iris moved carefully to the hump on the left side where the truck's body accommodated the back left wheel. She sat down and Arthur situated himself on the opposite hump. The truck bed was fairly clean. In the corner, to the right of Arthur there was a white bucket filled with cement crusted tools – wooden yard stick, a saw, steel brush, face mask and large pliers. A metal lunch pail, spade-headed shovel and a push broom lay next to the bucket.

It hadn't rained out there like it had in the city, the air dry and light, a gentle breeze slipping under Iris's skirt and Arthur's thin white shirt. The man-made lake settled into its nighttime ritual – the baritone croaks of bullfrogs and soprano cricket chirps mixed with lopping waves a few yards behind the tailgate. A crescent moon reflected off the water like a beam, that seemed to Arthur, to light only Iris's down-turned face.

Iris went into her purse and took out a pint of Seagram's gin. Arthur reached into the lunch pail next to him and pulled out a metal thermos.

He unscrewed the cap and wiped it against his blue pants before handing it to Iris. She poured herself a generous portion and handed the bottle to Arthur.

"To life," Iris said. They toasted, cap to bottle, and both took a deep swallow.

"It's so beautiful out here," she said.

Arthur nodded then looked past Iris, over her shoulder, into the blue-black that stood behind her like a screen. It was so dark that you couldn't tell the grass from the sky. He thought of being out in the country, about the wide, endless skies of Arkansas. For the first time in a long while, he smiled at the thought of home. A warmth settled in his chest that made him think of his mother, of family. He took quick glances at Iris, afraid to speak, scared of his thoughts and how they might come out. He wanted a family. He wanted a son. He wondered if his son would look like him, how it would feel to hold him against his chest, dark on dark, skin on skin, heart to heart. Love. He thought of love, what it would be like to be in love with Iris.

Iris saw him looking and looking away, like he was nervous. She smiled at the thought, amused that a man so tall, gruff, and strong could ever be skittish and uncomfortable. It all seemed so out of place. But then again, she was accustomed to things being out of place. She sipped her drink and thought about the way things were versus the way they should've been. Her mother shouldn't have died before she could memorize her face. She shouldn't have started her period so early. Her father shouldn't keep himself hidden away in his room, slowly and silently dying of sorrow and shame. And she shouldn't know the secret of Christine's oddity, a secret she often convinced herself was a dream, a nightmare.

A creaking bedroom door. Daddy coming into the room, shirtless and unapologetic, standing just inside the doorway, hands on his hips, chest heaving.

"Christine," he would whisper. "Christine, come see about your Daddy."

But most of all, she shouldn't be so hungry for freedom. Desire like hers was out of place, unnatural. Upturning roots, churning waters, and traveling to every corner of the earth, Iris wanted to be the wind. And she could be, she thought, if only someone would help her get free.

"What you thinkin' bout?" Arthur asked. His own voice sounded awkward in his ears. He wondered how he sounded to Iris. He brought the bottle of gin to his lips for a swig.

"You," Iris said.

"What about me?"

"You ain't so mean at all." Iris sipped and smiled.

Arthur looked at her. "Who said I was mean?"

"Everybody says you mean" Iris said. She drained her cup.

"Everybody, huh?" Arthur leaned forward and poured her some more.

"Everybody I've asked. Especially at Jimmy Cat's." Iris had never been to the bar, but had heard from her sisters that he was a regular there.

"So, you been to Jimmy Cat's askin' bout me?" He said calling her bluff. He raised the bottle and Iris lifted her cup.

The gin went down smooth and hot, with a cool echo that matched the minty scent of distant evergreens. They were both beginning to relax, settling into the ease of being with each other.

"Maybe," Iris said. She met his eyes and he didn't look away.

"Well, what you say?" Arthur asked. "You think I'm mean?"

"I just said you ain't so mean at all."

"There we go then." Arthur sat back. He set the gin bottle next to a bucket beside him.

"Why you suppose they say that? That you're mean?" Iris asked.

"Don't know. Don't care. Niggas, especially these uppity northern niggas say a lot of shit."

"What if I'm not talking about niggas?" Iris put her cup on the metal bed of the truck. "My sister said you were mean. Why would she say that? Was you mean to my sister, Arthur?"

Arthur chuckled. Iris got up and stepped forward. She placed her hands on his knees and knelt between them. She tilted her face towards his and he kissed her hard. She pulled away, licking her lips. She tasted gin, cigarettes, and salted potatoes.

"Naw, I wasn't mean to your sister." Arthur kissed Iris again lightly, grinning. "Your sister was mean to me."

"Oh, she was?" Iris nibbled his bottom lip, smirking seductively. They both avoided saying Christine's name, as if saying her name would conjure her up and she'd appear, in her haunting beauty, right there in the truck with them.

"I think maybe she just wasn't your kind of woman. Wasn't the kind of woman you wanted, the kind you need." Iris smiled and winked.

"And what do you know about the kind of woman I want? The kind I need?"

Arthur slid off the wheel hump and met Iris, both of them on their knees. He took her into his arms and kissed her neck. The bottle of gin spilled in the movement and the pungent liquor ran down the grooves of the truck bed.

There was no more conversation. There was just Iris and Arthur in the darkness, clutching each other in the back of the truck under the blackness of the night sky, warming each other with caresses and kisses. The stars looked down on them, throbbing in time with Arthur's heart and his aching for a home, pulsing to the rhythm of Iris's loins and her desire to be free. The came together, their bodies finding home in each other's movements, in each other's quickening breaths.

In the moments after, Iris lay with her head on Arthur's chest, smelling his cigarette smoke and sweat. She listened to his steady heartbeat against the sounds of restless frogs, crickets and water.

"Look at that," Iris said. She lifted her hand and pointed up to the sky. "Did you see that?"

Arthur didn't answer. He was staring at her hand, Iris's long, slender index finger pointing straight up and her other delicate fingers folded into a fist.

"I think it was a shooting star," she said. If it was, maybe it was a sign, a wink from God that she had found the man she had been looking for, the man that would emancipate her from the things she knew and embolden her to seek the things she didn't.

"Hold your hand just like that." Arthur's voice was low and sounded far away.

"Why? You missed it." Iris held her hand still.

Arthur stared up at Iris's hand for another moment before bringing it down to his mouth. He kissed the tip of her finger and closed his eyes.

"What Arthur?" Iris asked, snuggling beside his body, nuzzling her face into his neck.

He cleared his throat and placed Iris's hand on his chest lightly, thinking of his youth and briefly of home once more.

"Arthur?" Iris said again, an urgent need hiding between the sound of her voice and heat of her breath on his neck.

Arthur squeezed Iris closer to him, ready to share himself for what felt like the first time, ready to tell his story.

"There's this rock formation out in the Canary Islands that looks like a hand with an index finger pointing up at the sky. It's the craziest thing. I ain't never seen it for myself, but I would like to," he began. "See, I know rocks and earth…"

Iris closed her eyes and listened to Arthur tell his story. She let herself escape into his voice, into his life. She pictured a postcard. 'God's Finger is pointing at the sky here, hope God's face is smiling at you there,' she would write in her tiny, tight cursive.

They huddled together in the back of the truck until the sky began to lighten, talking and laughing. A mist rose up from the lake and a sharp, damp chill settled over everything. When Iris began to shiver and Arthur's lids felt heavy against his eyes, they readied themselves to go.

Arthur and Iris drove back to the city, their fingers intertwined. Their stomachs fluttered, knowing that they had just begun something special, neither of them considering that for every known thing there is an unknown.

Commitment Phobia

Denise didn't get a chance to sit down before Dr. Watson started the session. The good doctor skipped all the pleasantries. Sitting still and expectant at her desk, she asked, "What's keeping you from moving forward with your work? Is it the center? You still stuck on that story about the drug counselor, right? Are you sure you aren't basing that story on me?"

"Don't flatter yourself, Doc." Denise sat on the electric blue leather couch, then eased back to fully recline. The office was comfortable, soothing. The blue sofa providing a pop of color amid the varying shades of gray and white. Dr. Watson's glass-topped white desk and smoke-gray leather executive chair looked modern and sleek while the thick blue-speckled wool shag rug underneath offered the promise of warmth and softness. On the coin gray walls, black and white photos of children laughing, birds in flight, and snowcapped mountains lent themselves to quiet moments of reflection. Denise felt safe in Dr. Watson's office.

Denise exhaled loudly and rolled her shoulders as she looked down at her long legs, the bottoms of her jeans bunched around the top of leather boots. She thought about work, like it could be the reason her story had stalled. Denise was a program director at a small adult literacy center in

South Shore. She had started as a volunteer back in college but moved up once she had finished her English degree at NIU. Work at the center was fine. It was always fine. It wasn't that. "I've been stuck on that story for a while. It has nothing to do with my day job." she said. The deadline was looming. The anthology wanted her contribution before summer's end. Tulips along Michigan Avenue marked the start of spring, and she was nowhere near finishing the story about two women, Remy and Kat, who meet and fall in love at a blood drive though one of the women is hopelessly, yet secretly, in love with her drug counselor.

"Then what is it?" Dr. Watson said.

"Forget the story. I'm not here about that. I'm thinking of just ending it with a relapse anyway. The three of them have a coked-out orgy and start a commune in Mecca, Indiana."

"You don't have to be a smart-ass, Denise." Dr. Watson pursed her plum-colored lips. "Why are you here then?"

"I'm here to talk about Alesha."

"Let me re-phrase then. What's keeping you from moving forward with your relationship?"

"Fear." It came out automatically. Denise thought about it after she said it. One of her more notorious flaws—words came out; thoughts came later if at all.

Denise had been dating Alesha for seven months, a record for Denise. Her normal range for romantic entanglements was between two hours and three months. Somewhere around the 90-day mark, something or someone always happened and changed everything. But nothing had happened, and no one had taken Denise's attention, and for the first time in her life, she was completely into one woman. It was new for her, so she was taking it slow. Denise hadn't declared her love, hadn't pledged monogamy, and until recently, hadn't made even the faintest reference to a U-haul. They were playing it loose. Maybe that was the problem.

Dr. Watson, Denise's therapist for over a year, was silent. Denise settled herself on the couch and stared up at the ceiling. It was low and textured. She could never remember what it was called, but it was one of those wavy, swirled paint jobs that looked like frosting. Denise imagined reaching her arm up and out, like a Stretch Armstrong doll, and scooping a fingertip of ceiling. She wanted to taste it. She wondered if it would be grainy and syrupy-sweet like the frosting on supermarket birthday cakes or flat and salty-sweet like the dusty paint chips Denise used to eat as a kid. She had divulged her guilty childhood pleasure to Alesha one night. Alesha laughed and shook her head.

"Are you sure you ain't get lead poisoning?" she had said.

"I did not get lead poisoning," Denise said.

"You ever get tested?"

Denise scrunched her face. "I don't think so. I mean, I never told anyone I ate paint chips, so like..."

"Then how do you know?" Alesha raised an eyebrow then smiled.

Denise swallowed. "Oh shit." She ran a hand over her the tight curls of her closely-cropped hair.

Alesha had slapped Denise's shoulder and leaned into her for a kiss. "You're probably okay." She pressed her lips against Denise's lips, taking the bottom one between her teeth. She nibbled then pulled away. "Probably."

"Whose fear?" Dr. Watson said, interrupting Denise's memory.

Denise rolled the question around in her head. "Mine?" She winced at the inflection.

Dr. Watson made her scolding-disappointed sound. Tremolo and elastic, the guttural groan made Denise think of her mother. "Hmmmnnnnn."

Sliding her hands under her head and crossing her legs at the ankles, Denise licked her lips and asserted her answer. "Mine." she sank into the cushions of the couch at the admission. The cool leather sucked her down, swallowed her whole.

Denise wanted to be with Alesha. Really be with her. She wanted to wake up next to her every morning, breasts pressed against Alesha's warm, smooth back with the salty-sweet taste of pussy on her lips. She would cook a light breakfast of pancakes and fresh fruit. After eating, Denise would join her lover in the shower, who would then push her against the cool tile and play between her legs as they licked beads of water off each other's shoulders. In Denise's mind, it worked out perfectly. Conversations never dulled, passions never waned, and joys were never killed.

"You know you need to qualify that," Dr. Watson said.

"It's fear. My fear. Plain and simple. I feel agitated and worried."

"It's a long distance relationship," Dr. Watson noted, leaning back in her chair. "It's low pressure by nature. You are in your own space most of the time. And, other than being faithful in the meantime, what do you have to worry about?"

"I don't have a problem being faithful," Denise said, then thought about it. "I can be faithful. I'm faithful."

Dr. Watson narrowed her eyes. She scribbled a few notes.

"What?" Denise shrugged.

"Something must have happened. Did something happen?"

"No." Denise lied.

"What happened?"

"Nothing." Denise sighed and shifted on the couch.

The previous weekend, Denise had looked into Alesha's eyes, almond-shaped and dark as ink, and told her she loved her more than poetry.

Lucille Clifton, Nikki Giovanni, Audre Lorde, their lines meant nothing, stanzas shapeless and without life, rhythms lost and unheard against Alesha's beauty. Blasphemous? Denise didn't care. The urge to merge blew up inside her chest like a helium balloon. No, like a hot air balloon. No, a blimp; hard, metallic, explosive. Her chest threatened to burst at just the mere thought of Alesha, her smile, her smell, her skin.

"You should move in with me," Denise had said. They were lying naked on the living room floor. They tickled each other's palms, hypnotizing each other with touch. The stereo was on. Cassandra Wilson sang softly against tinkling piano keys and a whining saxophone. The sun had just cracked the horizon and Denise's apartment was bathed in a fuzzy blue, the corners of the room trying to hold on to the mystery of the night.

"Uh huh." Alesha bumped Denise's shoulder. "Why do you say things you don't mean?"

"I'm serious."

"No, you aren't," she had said cool and sure. She traced the lines on the inside of Denise's palm with her index finger.

Denise closed her hand on Alesha's finger, pulling her lover's hand to her mouth. Denise kissed the inside of her wrist and held her lips there. Denise could feel her pulse. Alesha pulled her hand away.

"What if I was?" The question implied that she wasn't. Denise chewed on her bottom lip and waited for Alesha to say something. Anything.

Alesha didn't respond. She rolled over onto her back. She stared at the ceiling and drummed her long fingers on her sternum. It made a hollow sound that seemed louder than it should have been.

Denise wasn't serious. She was just saying something to say something, suggesting and dreading in the same space. Another one of her flaws. Denise rolled onto her back too, secretly still waiting and, as always, thinking and thinking. The 'what-ifs' set in and Denise felt heat rise to her cheeks, prickling under her eyes. What if we feel smothered? What if we get bored? What if all we do is have sex all the time? What if we don't have sex enough? What if she meets someone else and has sex with them? What if I catch them? What if we struggle with bills? What if she expects too much? What if I'm not enough? What if I want more? What if I wake her with my nightmares, the way I call out sometimes or jump awake with a start? What if she can't get used to my late nights pounding away at the keyboard with a passion she hasn't felt in days?

Denise pictured Alesha stumbling into the kitchen, the only place she could work in peace once sharing her apartment. Alesha's short hair spiked on one side and matted on the other, hands on her hips, nipples screaming against her tank top. She would clear her throat, but Denise wouldn't respond until Alesha walked over and stood directly in front of her. She would take off her headphones, pull her glasses off and rub her tired eyes, the glare of her laptop and the lateness of the hour like gravel beneath her eyelids.

"You coming to bed?" Alesha would ask. And Denise wouldn't have an answer that would please her, every response too short, rude even.

"Eventually" or "I don't know. Maybe," or "Don't worry about me, go back to sleep." A dismissive flip of fingers, twisted lips and furrowed brows.

To her credit, Denise at least mentioned it, being together, sharing space. Alesha had kissed her and smiled. The smile, more like a smirk, said it all. It wasn't just Denise.

Alesha told Denise renting a car to drive from Chicago was a waste of money. So, Alesha drove her dusty Honda Civic up from East St. Louis every couple weeks. And although not in love with East St. Louis, she always called it 'home,' where good people made a way out of no way. Comparatively, Alesha thought Chicagoans—"no offense," she prefaced—were rude, obnoxious, full of perceived entitlement, and in too much of a hurry; "Why the hell does everyone have to walk so fucking fast?" she had asked once. "And where the fuck am I supposed to park?"

She knew Alesha would never bring up moving to Chicago on her own. So, Denise said it: Move in with me, instead of asking: Will you move in with me?

Alesha had pushed herself up from the floor. Her long legs on both sides of Denise and her toned arms folded across her chest: a woman warrior, an Amazon queen.

With her full lips fixed into a crooked grin, Alesha chuckled. "What am I going to do with you?"

At that moment, Denise hadn't the slightest idea and wasn't any closer to an answer sitting in Dr. Watson's office.

Denise exhaled too loud for it to mean nothing and heard Dr. Watson's chair squeak as she leaned back. Denise sat up.

"It is my fear, Doc. I can say that with no qualms. But," Denise raised an eyebrow and put up a finger to make her point. "Alesha takes solace in my cowardice." She nodded her head, trying to get Dr. Watson on board with her train of thought.

Dr. Watson leaned forward. She placed her elbows on the desk and rested her chin on her folded hands. Her face was thin, her cheek bones assertive; her hair was pulled into a tight ponytail at the base of her long neck. She was supportive but challenging, both best friend and greatest adversary. "Why do you say that?"

The doctor wasn't buying it. Denise stretched back out on the couch. Staring up at the ceiling made of frosting, Denise thought about what she had just said. She licked her lips at the thought of a creamy sweet ceiling, like maybe she could eat through it and be boundless.

"Tobias Stucco," Dr. Watson said. She stood up, walked around her desk. She leaned on the front of it and folded her arms across her chest. She wore a grey pin-striped pantsuit. Long and graceful, she looked more model than psychologist.

"Huh?" Denise sat up to face her.

Dr. Watson looked up at the ceiling then at Denise. "The paint. It's Tobias Stucco."

"You're good."

"I know," Dr. Watson said. "So, let's stop playing games. Why do you think Alesha takes... what did you say?" She looked down at her notes. "Why do you think she takes solace in your fear?"

Denise took one last glance at the ceiling. The mystique of the paint gone, she had no refuge. Staring down at her hands, she searched for a way out of the conversation.

"Because it's convenient. It only takes one of us to be scared. If I'm scared to take the next step, it stalls us. Her feelings don't even really matter." She shrugged. "You know what I mean?"

"Her feelings matter, Denise," Dr. Watson said.

Denise frowned.

"I'd like to see you take a chance. Challenge yourself." The doctor tapped her clipboard. "When will you see Alesha again?"

"Probably next week," Denise shrugged. "Or the week after."

"Good. That'll give you time to build your courage," Dr. Watson smiled. "Next time you see her, go with your gut the whole time. No matter what it is, take your initial thought, your first response, and go with it."

"But that's one of my problems," Denise stood up. "I'm always speaking before thinking, always—"

"No," Dr. Watson set her notes down. "That's not your problem. You pay me to tell you what your problems are."

Denise chuckled. "What's my problem then?"

The therapist perused her notes, smirking and flipping a few pages back and forth. She raised an eyebrow like she was unsure where to start.

"Damn. Am I that bad?"

"No. You're not bad at all. You're a good person who deserves good things."

Denise wasn't convinced.

"You need to believe that," Dr. Watson said. "You need to believe that you are a good person who deserves good things. Like happiness. Like love." She put her notebook down on her desk. "Listen to me. Trust yourself. Trust your gut. You know what you want. Go for it."

Denise nodded. "Trust my gut."

· · · ● · ● · · ·

Denise repeated 'trust my gut' like a mantra as she stepped off the train and walked the two blocks to her apartment. She turned the corner onto her block and stopped. On the concrete steps that lead to her building sat Alesha, an overstuffed duffle bag at her feet.

"What are you doing here?"

Alesha looked like she had been crying, her eyes puffy and red. She forced a smile.

"You still want me to move in with you?"

"Yes," Denise said. It came out fast and hard, certain and unafraid. She held out her hand and Alesha took it. They walked into the apartment building without talking, Denise carrying Alesha's bag in her right hand and squeezing Alesha's hand in her left.

Once inside the apartment, Alesha started to speak, but Denise put her finger over her lips. She walked Alesha towards the couch. They fell onto the tweed sofa, hands pulling at each other's clothes. When they finally undressed each other, Denise dove into Alesha face first and didn't stop until her lover's thighs quivered then shook then flexed then squeezed so tight they threatened to crush her skull.

"You want to tell me what happened?" Denise asked, out of breath. She lay between Alesha's legs, the slickness of their bodies like glue.

"The truth?" Alesha said. Her long fingers played in the soft coils of Denise's hair.

"Always."

Alesha's fingers stopped. "I don't want to talk about it to tell you what happened. I don't want to talk about it."

Denise met Alesha's eyes. She took a deep breath and pushed herself up until she was only inches from Alesha's face. "I'm glad you're here," she said.

The two women kissed. Sealing the conversation. That night, they made love all over the apartment, the both of them marking countertops, chairs, pillows, rugs, sinks, tables, walls, even the closets with their sweat, their cum. Everything shone in a different light, glimmered with new life; hers replaced by theirs.

· · • · • · • · · ·

"Long time no see," Dr. Watson said.

Denise flounced herself on the leather couch. The weather had gone from a sweet spring to a sweltering summer. Denise wore a purple tank top and ripped jeans. Gaping, fringe-lined holes exposed quick flashes of brown skin as she stretched out her legs.

"You look nice," Denise said, taking in her doctor's long legs as she leaned on the edge of her desk.

Dr. Watson cleared her throat. "Thank you." She smoothed her dress, a pale yellow strapless number with a thin, white patent leather belt that cinched her waist. "You haven't been in for a while. Seeing your name in my appointment book surprised me."

"I thought it might," Denise said.

"Denise, I cost too much for games. You know that."

"Yeah, I do." She shook her head.

"Well?" Dr. Watson sat on the edge of her desk and crossed her legs. She eyed her clipboard then looked at her patient, tilting her head. "How's the writing? You finish that story?"

Denise scowled and turned her head towards the back of the couch.

"I'll take that as a 'no.' What's the problem?"

"Not a damn thing," Denise said. She sat up, swinging her legs to the floor. Her Adidas slides slapped the hardwood floor. "Nothing's wrong. Everything's good. Too good."

"You've got to be kidding me." The doctor threw up her hands and walked around to her high-backed chair.

"No, no," Denise stood up. "For real. It's too... it's weird is what it is! Alesha cooks, she cleans, she runs me baths and... she gives me space. Even after sex. I leave her to go write and she smiles at me when I creep out of bed. She SMILES, Doc!"

Dr. Watson burst into laughter. It was a rich laughter, full of tumbling highs and lows. It made Denise think of rolling down a grassy hill full of fuzzy white dandelions.

"I'm serious." Denise smiled despite herself. "I'm going out of my mind. It's been two months and not a single fight, not a single disagreement."

"I don't believe that," Dr. Watson said, trying unsuccessfully to stifle her giggles.

"Okay, we argued very briefly over one thing."

"What?"

"Nothing. It doesn't even count."

Dr. Watson straightened her face. Her eyes were moist with amusement, her mouth waiting to crack a grin. "Tell me. What did you two fight about?"

"The bed." Denise rolled her eyes.

The therapist leaned forward. Her demeanor suddenly focused.

Embarrassed and annoyed, Denise told Dr. Watson how she likes to make her bed every morning. As obsessively compulsive as it sounded coming out of her mouth, the bed-making wasn't the issue. Alesha had no problem making the bed. She thought it made the room look neat; she thought Denise's insistence on making the bed was cute. The problem was how to make the bed.

"Alesha likes to tuck the sheet under at the foot of the bed. I don't. It makes it too tight when you get in. You can't move your legs freely. You can't kick off the sheets when it gets too warm. You can't..."

Dr. Watson covered her mouth.

"Go ahead. Laugh."

The doctor shook her head, her hand pressed against her face all the while. "You can't what?" Dr. Watson said, parting her fingers right at her lips. "Go ahead. I didn't mean to cut you off."

"You can't go to the bathroom, come back, climb into bed from the bottom and…"

"And what?"

Denise smacked her teeth. She collapsed onto the couch and threw her hands into the air. "There's no spontaneity. There's no… no passion! I knew this was going to happen. I knew it."

"Did you share this with Alesha?" Dr. Watson composed herself. She grabbed a pen from the collection of writing instruments held in a tall wooden cylinder, a topless woman, arms outstretched as if she was holding all the pens and pencils in her arms carved in front. Dr. Watson started writing.

"Yes. I mean, no." Denise covered her face with her hands. Quiet filled the room. "Something's just off. Like, things are great but also… something is just off." Denise peeked through her fingers and looked up at the ceiling, bored with it instantly. "How do you really know if you're sabotaging yourself or if something is really wrong when there's so much you don't know?"

"What do you mean?"

"She never told me why she was on my steps crying the day she came to live with me. I asked once, that first night. She didn't want to talk about it. I didn't press."

"There it is," Dr. Watson said. "That's what's troubling you. You need to ask her. And she needs to tell you."

"What if I don't like her answer?" Denise uncovered her face.

"Well, then you'll have a 'real' argument. Exactly what you want." Dr. Watson said matter-of-factly. "Exciting, yes?" She smiled.

·········

W hen Denise entered the apartment, the smell of fried fish enveloped her before she could toss her keys onto the table next to the door.

"Hey baby," Alesha called from the kitchen. Aretha Franklin's "Who's Zoomin' Who?" blared from the stereo; the standing fan whirled and ticked, ruffling the classifieds strewn across the cocktail table and sofa.

"Hey." Denise stood in the doorway of the kitchen. The windows were open, but the small space was stifling. Mixing bowls and assorted seasonings cluttered the round wooden table in the corner of the kitchen. Several of the overhead mahogany cabinets were open, and scattered vegetables filled the counter between the gas stove and small white refrigerator. Steam rose from a boiling pot of pasta and a simmering pan of red sauce. Denise watched her lover from behind.

Alesha was topless, but wore cut-off denim shorts and an apron. Her back shimmering. The small flock of black birds tattooed across her shoulder blade suspended in flight, the curve of her spine inviting. Alesha opened the fridge and pulled a Miller Light from the four pack on the nearly empty second shelf. She whirled around, kissed Denise on the cheek, and handed her the bottle of beer. Returning to the counter where she was chopping beef tomatoes for a salad, she spoke over her shoulder, barely turning her head.

"How was your day?"

"Fine. I, um, I... I didn't go into the center today." She used the bottom of her shirt to twist off the beer cap.

"No? What did you do with yourself all afternoon then?" She tossed the salad.

Denise watched Alesha's back muscles flex and release. She sipped from her bottle. "I ran errands. Went walking. I needed to think."

"I told you that story ending will come to you," Alesha said. She put the salad in the refrigerator, grabbed a beer for herself then leaned against the counter. Using the apron, she opened her bottle. She gulped from it hungrily, drinking the light beer like water. She exhaled and looked at the bottle as if during her guzzling it had transformed into something else, like the label might boast some magic recipe for livelihood and youth. "You've got all the elements... love triangle of sorts, or at least the potential for one, a big secret that everyone is waiting for... hell, I say find a way for Kat and the drug counselor to get together and call it a day. End it with a sex scene or something."

"Remy's the one seeing the counselor." Denise took a swig of her beer.

"I know," Alesha smiled. "That's what makes Kat fucking her all the more provocative." She winked.

Denise looked down at the floor.

"What's wrong with you?" Alesha asked. "If you're irritable because you're hungry, we can eat. The food is done."

"Why did you come here?" Denise stared at the floor.

"What?"

"Why are you here?" Denise looked into Alesha's eyes.

"I told you I didn't want to talk about it."

"I'm not asking you if you want to talk about it. I'm asking you to tell me about it. Why are you here? Why were you on my porch, bag in hand?" Denise clenched her fingers around her beer bottle.

Alesha turned and placed her bottle on the counter. A single drop of sweat ran down the middle of her back. Denise watched it approach the tie of the apron. She wondered if the tears in her lover's eyes were also falling.

"Are you sure you want to know?"

"Yes." Denise's body trembled. She felt her grip loosening, her muscles weakening.

"My girlfriend kicked me out when she found out about you," Alesha said.

·········

The office was silent save the sound of a light summer rain. Dr. Watson sat in her chair, clipboard in her lap, pen holding her hair in a small, twisted bun. She glanced over at Denise then returned her gaze to the window. Rain pelted lightly against the glass, the sky a pale, hopeful blue with low, malicious-looking grey clouds. Even the weather couldn't decide how to feel.

With her eyes closed, Denise finally broke the silence. She hadn't even said 'hello' when she came in twenty minutes before.

"The whole fucking time," she said in disbelief. "You know what this means, Doc."

"What does it mean, Denise?" Dr. Watson carefully selected a pen from the wooden woman's outstretched arms.

"It means I had every right to be apprehensive. My gut was telling me to be afraid, to be worried."

The psychologist scribbled notes on her clipboard. "Go on."

"Perhaps y'all doctors got it all wrong," Denise opened her eyes. The ceiling met her. She imagined it lowering, coming closer to her face until it rested a breath away from her lips. "Commitment-phobia isn't an irrational fear of love and connection. It isn't an aversion to stability and trust."

"Then what is it?" Dr. Watson asked. She made another note then tapped her pen against her chin, waiting.

"It's a hyper-awareness," Denise said. The ceiling moved closer still; she brushed the wavy surface of it with her lips when she spoke. "It's understanding that we only desire something when we can't have it. Sure, we want love, but once we get it...." Denise twisted her lips to the side and looked side-long at her therapist. "Commitment-phobes, of which you've certainly labeled me in your notes there, are the only people who really know and appreciate love. We live in the possibility of it, and it's thrilling."

Dr. Watson referenced an earlier page, made a note, and crossed her legs. "So once you actually have love, it loses its appeal? Love is best when it's a fantasy?"

"Exactly."

The ceiling pressed down upon Denise where she lay on the couch. She stuck her tongue out, slowly, touching the ceiling, tasting it. She pressed her tongue farther out, trying to push through it, but it wouldn't give. Licking the ceiling, she realized the texture and taste of it. It was not soft. It was not sweet.

The Liar

Opal was missing a finger. Well, not really missing it exactly. The pinky on her right hand was a nub. It stopped short, ended just at what would have been the second knuckle of her three jointed appendage. Instead, she had a stump of bone, flesh and skin—no nail—that ended in a smooth roundness that tingled when rubbed directly. As far as she knew, she was born that way. She remembers doctors, therapists, teachers, and foster mothers trying to get her to write with her left hand, but she refused. As a result, she only wrote with short, stubby pencils that she held like tiny pieces of chalk, with bunched fingertips; her thumb, index, middle, and ring fingers went pale in the fierceness of her grip. Her hand hovered directly over the paper, no slant, pencil tip straight against the pages of her journal as she wrote entries that would have a hard time becoming stories.

Opal never revealed the real story of her pinky—or lack thereof—to anyone. When asked, about her finger or her mother, she always found it more interesting, and in the end much safer, to lie.

Opal told people her mother's name was Lillie, a name Opal chose after reading *The Temple of My Familiar* for the ninth time. The name was the first lie of many that would follow. In most stories, Lillie died when Opal was a baby. Opal was then "tolerated"—as she liked to say—across foster homes until she turned eighteen.

Stretching the truth when necessary and downright inventing it when required allowed Opal to feel in control of her story, in control of her very being. She knew that one's personal story held a special power, a power that could invite people closer or push them away. She wanted to be in control of that power always, especially when dealing with how, when, where, and if she shared her heart.

When Opal took lovers, which she did liberally, she told them different stories about her mother and about her finger. The lovers marveled at the story, trying not to look at the nub as Opal spoke. They stared directly into her large brown eyes that always seemed to be shiny with impending tears, a characteristic that complemented the storytelling because it made her look sincere. The listening lover, whether self-proclaimed or closeted freak, would take Opal's hand gently and kiss the soft round stump of her last digit, sending a lightning bolt of tingling arousal to flip and swirl and flutter between her legs. Some lovers, the more adventurous ones, begged Opal to pleasure them with her nub, hurriedly pushing her hand between their legs before she had even finished the story.

Opal told January, a journalism student at UIC, that she lost her pinky in an unfortunate door slamming incident. The heavy, rusted passenger door of a 1985 Mercury Marquis clamped Opal's five-year old finger like a bear trap, and in a panic of pain and surprise, she yanked away, jerking her hand up and out, the top portion of her pinky left inside the door. Yes, even as a child, Opal purported herself to be that strong. She told Marisol, a woman who'd only dreamt of snow until arriving at University of Chicago, that she lost her finger to frostbite, a wicked case that turned her finger tips from brown to red to yellow to white then blue to black. The doctors could save them all except one. Opal told Marisol, "Don't buy gloves. Always get mittens. The fingers need to be together to truly stay warm."

Tomorrow, a single mother going into social work, got a story about a knife fight that went down at one of Opal's foster homes. For Mina, a factory accident working for a meat-packing company in Melrose Park. Kimora, a tale of a careless slicing accident from Opal's days working at a deli; "To this day, I don't fuck with Pastrami," she had said. For Daesha, sweet, sweet Daesha, who was studying for her GED, Opal imparted a story about getting distracted by a fight that broke out in a high school wood shop class and how the buster ass shop teacher, Mr. Kuklah, gave her an 'F' because she didn't finish her birdhouse, never mind the band saw that severed half her pinky in an even cut worthy of an 'A.

Unlike her lovers, Opal recycled her stories. She changed tiny details – the make and model of the car—'81 Cadillac Seville, '78 Olds Cutlass, '85 Buick Skylark; the name and location of the deli—Ada's on Wabash, the Riverside on Cortland, even the Subway out by Ford City Mall; the woodshop project—spice rack, lazy susan, lamp. The only details that never changed were the hospital, Cook County Emergency, where she sat bleeding down her arm, shirt front, lap and floor until they finally called her name, and of course, the imminent loss of half of her pinky finger.

The love affair would end shortly after the storytelling. Something about the woman asking about the finger coinciding with a shift in the lovemaking from the figurative to the presumed literal. And perhaps that's what made Cree different.

Cree and Opal met at the Checkerboard in Hyde Park. It was a Blues club, at the time too big for its own good, the small, empty tables a reminder of better days. With tea lights as centerpieces, the dark club was like its own universe, candles like intermittent stars, lonely suns with no planets in orbit. There were a few regulars at the far end of the bar, sipping Hennessy or Crown, bodies slumped on stools. A few couples hunched over the small tables near the stage, whispering and bouncing their legs under the white table cloths. After a song or two from the band, at least one couple would courageously make their way to the shiny, wooden dance floor to two-step the night away. Opal always went on Thursday nights and sat to the right of the stage, or stage left as Cree would correct her later, and watched the faces of everyone in the band. The bass player thumped his strings with his eyes closed, and the drummer held his bottom lip between his crooked teeth as he attacked the snare and the high-hat. The lead singer, Lizz, caressed the microphone as if stroking a lover and sang with the voices of women long gone, women that made Opal wish she was from another time: Bessie Smith, Ma Rainey, and Nina Simone. Then, there was Cree on guitar.

Cree's guitar, a hollow body made for the Blues, was the shiny, deep purple of a grape Jolly Rancher and just as sweet. It wailed, whispered, and whined as Cree's fingers slid up and down the frets. Opal was mesmerized by the way Cree's fingers moved. She fantasized about how they would feel on her skin, the callused fingertips, short nails, and what she imagined to be soft, warm palms. Cree broke into a solo that twisted and turned so slowly on itself it forced Opal to cross her legs. She took Cree in from blown-out afro to thick-soled, scuffed, black leather boots. Cree held her guitar close to her, a swell of breast drooping over the curvature of the guitar's wide, glossy body. Opal imagined being on top of her and smirked at the thought of requesting, mouth hot and voice husky in Cree's ear, that she keep her boots on.

Though Cree said she had noticed Opal from the first moment she saw her, it took them a month of Thursdays to finally speak to one another.

After the show, Opal made her way to the parking lot behind the club. Shivering from a light drizzle that made the air heavy with the threat of cold rain, she waited for Cree. Opal buttoned up her peacoat. The band members finally came ambling out the door and down the small steps, exchanging hugs before dashing from under the awning to their cars. Lizz and Cree came walking out together, arm-in-arm. Opal's heart popped and went dark, a blown light bulb. When Lizz and Cree reached the parking lot, Opal's new idea was to compliment the band and be on her way. Lizz slipped her arm from Cree's and twisted her lips at Opal.

"I enjoyed you tonight," Opal said to Lizz and Cree.

"Thank you," Cree said.

"Huh uh," Lizz grunted before whispering into Cree's ear. Cree said she was fine and kissed Lizz on the cheek. Lizz offered Opal a phony smile and turned on her heels, clicking toward her car.

"What's with her?" Opal asked.

"Lizz is cool. She's just a little over-protective of me sometimes. I usually get a ride home with her. And..." Cree shuffled her guitar case to her left hand, "she's always suspicious of groupies."

"So, I'm a groupie?"

"I don't know yet." Cree narrowed her eyes. "You waited out here just to compliment the band?"

"Yeah," Opal said. "That, and I was hoping you'd take me home with you."

Cree's eyes widened. "You're bold."

"What kind of groupie would I be if I weren't?"

"What's your name?"

"Opal."

"Well, Opal, you caught me on a rare night. Come on."

Opal and Cree walked to the bus stop. They exchanged small talk as new acquaintances do, small silences filled with the crunching of gravel underfoot and the awkward chuckles of two people both anxious and nervous about the coming night. They compared zodiac signs: Cree's Ram to Opal's Virgin. They shared aspirations: Cree, record an album of original songs; Opal, finish a novel-in-stories. They sighed about the banality of making ends meet: Cree, part-time at the Wine Warehouse and Opal, unemployed, living off school loans while barely attending classes at Columbia.

"We're both in the South Loop," they said in unison.

When the number 14 bus arrived, Opal stood back and let Cree board ahead of her. Slyly, she hoped, Opal smelled Cree's hair. Lilac and cigarettes.

The bus zoomed up Jeffery, the streets quiet and wet. When they made it to South Shore, both Cree and Opal pointed out the Jeffery Pub as they passed it. Thinking forward, they made a date to go there on Saturday. Cree pulled the cord for 75th street.

Cree and Opal stepped off the bus and back into the cold, wet air. The bus revved then hissed off, exhaust billowing where Opal and Cree stood.

They walked wordlessly to Cree's apartment, a foreboding, four-story brick building with creaking wooden stairs and no elevator. Over their hard, hollow footfalls, Opal could hear Cree's breath. She wanted to feel it, hot and wanting, hovering in the space between her lips before a kiss.

Once inside, Cree lit every candle she owned while Opal was in the bathroom. They sat on the floor in the living room, surrounded by pillows and waltzing shadows, and drank Sherry. Cree played a song she had written, the electric guitar sounding metallic and stiff without the amp, and Opal, sliding a Sanchez book from a leaning stack of titles in front of a book shelf, read her favorite haikus aloud.

The sun was slowly pushing up from the horizon when Opal finally, and gently, pushed Cree down on the pillows that were gathered on the floor. They kissed, touched, and exchanged breath and sweat in ways so bold and rare, they came together in a burst of blinding purple light not caring if they ever saw each other again.

While Cree was sleeping, Opal crept out. It was just after noon. When she got home, she took a pencil stub and her journal into the kitchen. She wrote about a woman and her lover. She used the name Cree because after the morning's love-making, it seemed to be the only name her tongue ever knew.

· · • • · • · · · ·

Baptism

By Opal

Nearly every Sunday, Cree and I take a bath together. She picks the music and I run the water. In the kitchen, Cree makes cocktails. I can hear the sigh of the freezer, clink of ice, and Cree singing along with Cassandra Wilson as she pours. I test the water. Dipping a toe, submerging a foot, the steam making the hair on my legs curl. I slide my body into the water and lean back; the steaming water makes islands of my breasts.

Cree enters, naked. Passes me drinks and I place them on the windowsill. Cree sits on the covered toilet, lights a cigarette and smokes, the corners of her mouth curl into a grin.

"One day, you're going to boil the flesh right off your bones."

I love it when she's morbid. I laugh. She puts out her cigarette and comes close. Cree lifts her legs over the lip of the tub and stands between my legs. Her breath coming out in gasps, she folds herself down between my thighs. When she finally touches me, I am slippery and hot against her fingertips. She makes me feel unique.

· · • · • · • · • · ·

Cree went to Opal's tiny, Hyde Park apartment after working the Friday wine tasting. They made love on Opal's futon with an immediacy so severe that there was no time to recline it. Upright and out of breath, they sat tickling each other's palms.

"Aren't you curious?" Opal asked, tracing Cree's lifeline with her nub.

"I was," Cree said, grabbing Opal's hand and kissing the tip each of her fingers and the stump of her pinky, sending the tremors to where they were needed most. "At first."

"Then?"

"It passed."

Opal frowned. Stunned.

"You look disappointed. Do you want me to ask about it?"

"No," Opal shrugged. "I mean, yes."

"Why?"

"So, I can have the opportunity to finally tell the truth."

"The truth doesn't need opportunity. It just is."

Opal felt a shift, and it scared her. She got up and grabbed her journal. She read "Baptism" to Cree. It was the first time she had ever shared anything from her journal with anyone.

Cree gave her a suggestion. "Mention something about the hiss of the bus rolling past. I like that sound. I can hear it in my apartment."

Opal smiled. "That's a good idea." Cree put her head in Opal's lap. Opal looked down at her. "My muse."

"I have a boyfriend," Cree said.

No opportunity needed.

· · • • · • · · · ·

Jeffery Pub looked small from the outside, easily missed even with the neon rainbow hanging in the first of two dark windows. Once inside, the place opened up, wide and deep, the mood dark and warm like walking inside a hungry mouth. The defiance of Jeffery's Pub was palpable, an actual force that held up the walls and made the floor solid. The resiliency of having survived infused Opal with a sense of challenge as she settled on a stool scratchy with cracked vinyl. Opal looked over her shoulder at the sparse crowd, a private party clustered together in one corner, the shine of their Mylar balloons swallowed by shadows.

Opal sipped her Guinness and watched the door. She had kicked Cree out after her announcement, but as she had watched her walking up the street, she had fought the urge to raise the window and call after her. She didn't care that Cree had a boyfriend but cared that she had a *boyfriend*, a somebody that wasn't her, but to tell her that meant to say, directly and honestly, that she wanted Cree all to herself. She drank more of her beer, taking long, thirsty gulps, unsure if she was upset about the truth or the missed opportunity to tell it.

"The truth doesn't need an opportunity," she whispered to herself before draining the last of her beer.

As she hoped, Cree entered, unbuttoning her jacket and unraveling a long, red and black scarf that wrapped around her neck more than twice. Opal waited until Cree took a seat at the far end of the bar before going over to her.

"Dump him," Opal said.

Cree laughed. "Okay."

They ran the few blocks to Cree's apartment and kissed each other roughly at each corner before crossing the street. Once inside Cree's apartment, they fumbled with coats, scarves, and belts as they clamored up the stairs. After making love on the floor in Cree's bedroom, they listened to the streets and fucked again and again with each passing bus.

· · · · ● · ● · · · ·

Cree's grandfather, who lived in Milwaukee, was dying.

"I need you," Cree said. "Can you come tomorrow morning? I'll wait for you at the train station."

"Yes," Opal said.

Opal hung up the phone and finished sharpening her pencils. Sitting alone in the apartment, Opal thought about death, thinking maybe she could write a story about it. Her journal on her lap as she sat on the floor of her warm apartment, her tiny pencil gripped between her fingertips, she whispered the name 'Jocelyn' before writing it on the top of her page.

Jocelyn, a girl Opal had gone to high school with, had been killed two weeks before Christmas break during her junior year. It had been a stray bullet, a searing point of destruction that moved quick and resolute, though it had no eyes, no ears, no mind.

Opal drew a line under Jocelyn's name. She hadn't really known Jocelyn, but she remembered watching her and thinking she was beautiful and fearless. She remembered Jocelyn popping her gum and patting her braids to quell the itch of her scalp. Opal always saw her in the cafeteria, laughing a big, carefree laugh that sounded too large for her small frame. She cussed just as boldly, 'fuck that' and 'fuck this' and 'fuck you,' and she ate a bag of Flaming Hot Cheetos for lunch every day.

There had been a candlelight vigil in front of the school. There was singing and crying. The superintendent said a few kind, but superficial, words before hugging Jocelyn's mother awkwardly. There was a white ribbon tied around every tree that lined the block between West Normal and South Normal, the irony of the intersection going ignored. The flag was lowered half-staff, and the rest of the week was solemn. The table Jocelyn used to eat at with her friends was quiet for a few weeks. All of Jocelyn's friends ate their Cheetos in slow motion, sucking them rather than munching, forcing swallows rather than smacking. By Christmas break, Opal felt a normalcy creeping back into the school routine and wondered if anyone else felt guilty.

Classes resumed in the New Year and though something had definitely shifted, everything had settled into its new place. Opal still listened for Jocelyn's laugh and watched the lunch table like maybe one day she would show up, patting her braids and popping her gum.

Opal read over Jocelyn's name. She went to the next line and started writing. She wrote and wrote, her hand aching. She fell asleep mid-sentence and woke up to a dark apartment. It was a quarter after five.

· · · **·** · **·** · · ·

Death

By Opal

Jocelyn

Death is a cold certainty that hardens and sharpens you, coal into dia-mond. Death is death is death is death is death is

Death is.

I remember being born. The warmth of my mother. The violence of being expelled. Squeezed, pushed, pulled, twisted, and turned. Metal clamping my head. Skin tearing around me. Screams. Moans. Sobs. Voices. Soft, hushed, muffled in layers of flesh and fluid. A rush of air colliding with my skin so brutally, so cold and absolute. The black burned into red. Frantic hands slipping against my skin. Tenderness. Pain. The ridges of fingerprints, the lines of palms like steel wool. Fingers in my nose and mouth. I gag. I scream. My voice a surprising horror to my own ears.

The warmth, the voice, gone.

A diamond remains?

········•·••··

Cree broke up with Opal for not coming to Milwaukee. She did it over the phone, saying she never wanted to see her again. She then paused, breathing heavy and slow.

"I needed you," Cree said.

Opal knew it. "I wanted to be there for you but..." Should she lie? Tell the truth? What was the truth? Did she deliberately oversleep or was the remembering an exhaustion that covered her with a blanket of sadness too heavy to lift?

"But what, Opal? But what?"

"I was afraid."

Cree sighed then hung up the phone.

·····•·••··

Three Words

By Opal

Body covered in diamond dust from the wearing down, the grinding, the carving. My skin catches light only to shoot it out of my pores. I touch and kiss and lick and bite and leave streaks of rainbow on my lovers' skin. I have nothing to say, only things to show you. Look at the colors that bleed through the sheets when we make love.

Those three little words: I am scared. I love you. I am scared. I love you. I am scared. I love you.

· · • · • · • · · ·

Opal decided her heart was just as stumped as her pinky but wondered if it had to be a permanent condition. She called Cree every day. Cree never answered. She went to the Checkerboard, and when Cree took the stage, she turned her back to Opal, to the left or right, giving nothing. When Opal sat in the center of the audience, resting her arms on a table made level with sugar packets, Cree turned her back to the entire bar, riffing and tearing into urgent, jagged solos that caught the band off-guard. Opal would leave before the set ended, frustrated and irritated with herself. She didn't have a plan. Didn't know what she wanted to say.

· · • · • · • · · ·

Untitled

By Opal

I don't remember how I lost my pinky. I don't know if I was born this way or if something happened in the spaces between being born and the void that my mother became. I remember being born though, which I've heard is weird as shit. I can describe it. The being inside. The warmth of the darkness, the safety of it. Then the jolt and shock of cold and bright, the pain of pull and pinch. I've never told anyone this but I am telling you.

My mother died before I could know her. My mind holds flashes of sleeping with her in temporary rooms, the walls changing, the smells always in flux. Smells that I had no words for and voices that belonged to people whose names I will never know. There is a coldness to her skin in one of my memories, a light gone out of her eyes and a low whirl that I know now was ceiling fan, a smell that I know now was smoke. The sound of a fan where the sound of her breath should have been. The smell of smoke where her sweat and sweet should have been. I've never told anyone this but I am telling you.

I used to practice remembering. I would close my eyes and sit alone in whatever room I was assigned, lay awake but silent in whatever bed I was given, and try to remember. Only flashes come. Impressions and reflections. So, I make things up. I retell my story in ways that fit the moment or fit my intentions, to stay or to leave. I can always tell a story. I can always imagine and recall as if fact, as if evidence of things that definitely-probably-could-be-are-and-was. I am a liar. I've never told anyone this but I am telling you.

My favorite lie to tell is the one I tell myself. I tell myself that I am special. I tell myself that I am a bright, shining diamond. I am strong. I am beautiful.

I am not a diamond. I am just me.

I am afraid that being me is not good enough.

I have never told anyone this but I am telling you.

'I am afraid' feels more intimate, feels more true, feels more open, than saying 'I love you.' Or maybe for me, they mean the same thing.

I am afraid. I have never told anyone this but I am telling you.

I love you. I have never told anyone this but I am telling you.

· · · ● ● · ● · · ·

Opal didn't go inside. She stood outside the whole time. She waited in the parking lot beneath a light post near Lizz's car and practiced remembering. She didn't try to remember the past. She tried to recall every moment with Cree without mixing them with imaginings and hopes and fears. She tried to remember what she really said and not what she had wished she said, what really happened and not what she hoped or feared would happen.

The bass player came out first, his arm around a woman with braids that nearly swept the concrete. He tossed a "good night y'all" over his shoulder as the rest of the band entered the night. The drummer, alone for once, searched his pockets as he walked down the short set of stairs. When his pudgy hand emerged, it held a bent Black and Mild. He shrugged and went to light it anyway. He squinted through the smoke and nodded his head in Opal's direction before heading to his truck. Lizz and Cree came out last, arm in arm, Cree's head resting on Lizz's shoulder.

Opal stepped forward but didn't say anything.

Lizz shook her head and held up her hand. "Don't even think about it."

Cree lifted her head and slipped her arm from Lizz. She stared at Opal then twisted her lips to the side before turning her back to Opal. "Leave." She said it loud. Almost yelled it.

"I just want to give you something, Cree. That's all. I just... can I give you something? Something I wrote?"

Lizz walked up on Opal, ignoring the folded paper she held in her hand. "Look bitch, she ain't interested." She flipped her fingers at the paper.

"Whatever the fuck this is, some apology letter or poem, she don't want it."

Cree didn't turn. She kept facing the building. Her arms at her side and her hands clenched into fists, she took deep breaths. Opal noticed it, the breaths, so deep and slow they raised Cree's shoulders and straightened her back. She was fighting the urge to turn around. She was working hard to keep her resolve. Opal didn't know how she knew this exactly but she did. Opal and Cree, polar opposites of effort. A struggle to open met with a struggle to close, both of them losing.

"It's not a letter. It's not a poem. I don't know what it is." Opal looked down at the paper in her hand. "It's the truth. Maybe that's why it feels so unfamiliar."

Cree turned to Opal. She glanced at the paper then looked deep into Opal's eyes. "Leave," she said.

"Please," Opal said. "Please take this. Read it whenever. Or don't. I need to give it to you. No matter what you do with it, I need to try. I've never tried before. Not like this."

Cree sighed and looked up at the sky. Opal wondered if she was praying. She looked up, too. The sky was beautiful, blue-black with purple clouds strewn across it like tulle.

Lizz huffed and turned on her heels, headed to the car. Walking hard, she cursed under her breath as she unlocked the car. She shook her head and called out to Cree from the open driver's side door. "You coming or not?"

"I'm coming," Cree said. She blew out a breath and snatched the paper from Opal's outstretched hand. She walked to the car without turning around.

· · · ● · ● · · ·

The bath had turned cold but Opal couldn't bring herself to get out just yet. She drank the last of her tepid beer, stretched to place the bottle on the window seal and contemplated her hands. She spread her fingers out in front of her. She stared at her nub of pinky then closed her eyes. For the last month, she hadn't been able to write. She had attempted a short story and played around with a few lines that wanted to be a poem but didn't quite come together. She had made a list of all the pinky stories she had told then spent hours on end trying to remember the first time she ever noticed her fingers and toes. As she sank into the cool water, she thought about when babies discover their fingers and toes. How at some point, they pull their feet into their mouths and marvel at their own grasp around the flesh of their mother's finger or the skin of their mother's breast. It didn't seem to be a recognition of digits as much as a realization of stretch and grab, of reach and hold.

A knock on the door interrupted her thoughts. She sat up, heart thumping in time with the drip from the sink and just as loud. She pushed herself up slowly from the water and grabbed her towel from the doorknob. There were two more knocks, hard and deliberate. Urgent even.

Opal looked into the peep hole then opened the door so fast her towel drooped in the effort. She grasped it around her, adjusting it across her breasts and holding it against her chest.

Cree stood back from the door. Her hair wide and glorious, a halo. Her lips, slightly parted as if she was about to say something but wasn't sure what, looked fuller and softer than Opal remembered; everything about her more beautiful than Opal remembered. Perhaps that was the point. Maybe that was the lesson of it all, that nothing is more beautiful than now.

Opal cinched her towel at her chest. "I'm glad you—"

"Opal." Cree pulled the crumpled paper from the back pocket of her jeans. She unfolded it and smoothed it between her hands. "You are not a diamond. You are Opal." She stepped forward into the apartment. Opal took a step back, letting Cree inside.

"You are Opal," Cree said again as she closed the door behind her.

Baby Girl

1. My mother called me this morning, from Jacksonville, Florida, where I used to live before graduating from college and joining a very problematic "Teach for America," which landed me in Chicago, Illinois. My mother sang to me, voice energetic and happy, a faster, more creative version of the "Happy Birthday" Song. Thank you, Stevie Wonder.

2. I'm twenty-eight today and have celebrated my birthday the same way for the last ten years. So, as is tradition, by 11 p.m. I will be too drunk to stand.

3. My father hasn't called me on my birthday since he and my mother legally separated—a faster, less expensive version of divorce—when I was sixteen years old.

4. I lied in number two. Last year, I didn't celebrate my birthday.

5. As a kid, when I got into trouble, my mama took to my ass with my father's thick black leather belt. My mama told my father, "Stealing and lying. Toya gets that shit from you." My father would raise his ashy, construction worker hands and say, "Hey now. Mama's baby, Daddy's maybe."

6. (re: Number 4) Two weeks before my 27th birthday, I came home to Petra, my lover of ten months, sitting at the kitchen table, her

blond-streaked afro matted on one side from lying in bed crying all day. Staring at her hands, she told me she was pregnant.

7. It is absolutely impossible that Petra's baby is mine.

8. I arrived at the bar to meet friends at 8 p.m. My two best friends showed up, both fellow teachers. Ginny taught 3rd grade and Michelle 5th grade like me. We started the night with shots: Three Patron shots for my birthday, one Yager shot for the in-service that gave us tomorrow off, and two shots of Maker's Mark for death to No Child Left Behind.

9. While ordering a Red Stripe, my phone rang. It was Petra. I didn't answer. My phone vibrated once. She left a message.

10. I drank four and a half beers before having to take a piss.

11. Inside the bathroom, I listened to Petra's message. The birthday song. Her voice soft as cotton balls falling to the floor. My eyes watered. A baby giggled in the background. I deleted the message.

12. Number 10 is a new record.

13. It was 10:49 when I started alternately zoning out and winking across the bar at a woman with wavy brown hair and skin the color of the Sahara Desert. She sent me a shot of Patron. I winked at her once more, slammed the tequila then blew her a kiss. She blushed.

14. When I was 9 years old, I watched my father drink a half-pint of Erk & Jerk in 10 seconds. I remember counting his gulps—one per second and the brandy was gone. Leaving the alley behind the liquor store, we staggered; him from the drink and me from his weight on my bony shoulders.

15. When Petra told me she was bisexual, it didn't bother me like it did some of my friends. Being with her made me feel special, bigger and better than I really was. She encouraged me to leave my comfort zone, inspired me to try new things and loose myself from other people's expectations.

16. I have no memory of leaving the bar.

17. That day in the kitchen, Petra had tried to explain. She cried and rambled while packing her shit. She was sorry. It was an old friend that happened to be in town. They caught up. "I've got a wife and two kids," he had said. "I've got a girlfriend," she had said. They toasted to "Expectations" and got drunk. In the moment, I couldn't find any words, so I left. Instead of celebrating my birthday by getting staggering drunk, I pushed everything out of my mind by getting raging drunk, pointing and yelling drunk, crying and screaming drunk. At some point during our argument when I got home, I called Petra a bitch. She looked at me like I had slapped her.

18. The day after my birthday, I woke up next to the woman with the Sahara skin. I tried to remember her name. The only thing on the tip of my tongue was the sharp bittersweet twang of limes. "I need to go," I said. "No," she whispered with an accent that made me think of maracas. She stretched across me and said, "I want you to stay forever." I smiled, sliding from beneath her.

19. Petra has written me letters every two weeks since we broke up. I think she writes them when she's drunk because of the way her words slant off the page. I read them as soon as they arrive then stash them in an old Timberlands box under my bed. A whole year of rambling letters that never make any sense. "Sorry, you can't breathe. Regret is your mother. Pain is good."

20. My father has other kids. Boys from a previous marriage and a daughter in Ohio, who found my number a few years ago and called me. Her name is Veronica. "You ever think of your other kids?" I asked my father one day. He sighed into the phone. "The girl sends me cards sometimes." He never says her name. I try to remember the last time he's said mine.

21. I shouldn't have to try.

22. Walking to the Blue Line train, my father called. His voice was thick, like his mouth was stuffed with salt-water taffy. "Happy birthday," he said. "Thanks," I answered. "Only a day late this time, old man. Not bad," I added. He didn't hear me. "How old is you now? Thirty, right? Shit, my baby girl done got grown on her old man. You still love me, baby girl?" I told him yes. He said, "That's good." We hung up.

23. I am my father's daughter. I am Daddy's baby girl.

24. Once home, I sat in the middle of my living room floor with a cup of coffee, no Bailey's, Amaretto or Kahlua, just coffee, and I pulled out the Timberland box and re-read all of Petra's letters. I had really only read them when I was drunk. I can tell because the letters were neat and beautifully curled at the ends with heart-squeezing sentences. "Without you I can't breathe. My regret twists and turns in my stomach, squeezes it. I worry the pressure, the pain, will hurt the baby, and I want so much to be a good mother. I know I can be a good mother. I think you could, too." I read the last letter. She'd had the baby. It was a girl. I ran my fingers over the letters of her name like it was Braille.

25. I called Petra.

26. She answered on the fourth ring. "Hey," I said. "Toya?" she said. "Yeah. It's me. What's up?" It was silent for ten seconds. I counted with heartbeats. "Um, nothing," Petra said. "I'm just... I'm at home and... I'm... is everything all right? I can't believe you're calling me... I don't know what to say." I took a deep breath. "Look," I exhaled quickly, wincing as I continued. "Why don't you come over so we can talk. We've made mistakes, but I think... we can find our way back."

27. "You sure?" Petra asked. We both held our breath. In the space between, I decided that I would celebrate my birthdays differently, that

I would be different. Petra broke the silence. "I don't have anybody to watch—," she said. "Felicia," we said in unison.

28. "Bring her," I said. "Bring her."

We Call Love Longed For

When Bernadette got to Jimmy Cat's place, it was nearly empty. Jimmy sat in the corner booth counting money. Two men in shiny black slacks and crumpled shirts sat at the bar. They sat loose, almost dripping off their stools, their hands limply curled around half-empty glasses of beer, which looked stale and settled like sample jars of piss.

Bernadette nodded at Jimmy and went down to the far end of the bar. Gloria, the bartender, saw her coming and smiled. Flipping a dingy cloth across her shoulder, she reached under the bar and grabbed two shot glasses. Bernadette, her shoulders broad and her hair cut into a short, militant afro, slid her tall body onto the cool, black stool directly in front of her.

"You ain't been down here past the witching hour in a long while. Who you been hiding in?" Gloria chuckled through closed teeth with a hiss. She thought it downplayed the size of her mouth, which was wide with large pink gums and tiny teeth.

"I'm not fooling with you tonight, Miss Gloria," Bernadette said. She watched Gloria fill the two shot glasses with Johnny Walker and set the bottle down. Gloria slid one shot to Bernadette and lifted the other.

The two women, friends since Lincoln Middle School, nodded at one another before knocking the shots back and slamming the empty glasses on the bar. Gloria smiled and refilled the glasses. They repeated the quick drink and Bernadette shivered despite herself.

"You ain't getting old on me is you Miss Bernadette?" Gloria flipped her hair and poured two more shots.

Bernadette grabbed the shot glass. "You're getting old. I'm getting better." She raised the glass to Gloria and held it to her lips. Her friend followed suit, and they slammed the drinks once more.

"I know when you come in here after two a.m. you looking for more than whiskey to wet your tongue." Gloria put the Walker away and spun around to the dented, white cooler behind her. She took out a can of Pabst, popped it, and slid it to Bernadette.

"I don't get a glass?" Bernadette leaned forward on the bar to scoot her stool closer.

"Oh, you want a glass tonight, huh?"

"What's that shit your mama used to say? 'A woman ain't nothing unless she's a lady,'" Bernadette rolled her eyes and chuckled softly.

"You know that was her way of fuckin' with you." Gloria laughed, too. "Lady this and lady that. That woman…"

"Let's not conjure her up. She liable to raise up from the ground and grab us both by our collars." Bernadette shuddered at the memory of Gloria's stern, unrelenting mother, Mrs. Roundtree. Mrs. Roundtree didn't take too kindly to Bernadette and Gloria spending time together. According to her, Bernadette was a bad influence on her "little angel" but it was actually the other way around. It was Gloria who stole cigarettes from her father's jacket and albums from Diggy's record store. It was Gloria who encouraged Bernadette to skip classes and sneak into movies. It was Gloria who, on one cold, quiet Saturday night while her parents were out for the evening, invited Bernadette into her bedroom and taught her how to kiss.

"You right about that," Gloria said.

"Speaking of ladies, though…" Bernadette looked around the bar.

"Uh huh." Gloria tilted a pint glass and poured the beer slowly. "Only lady here for you tonight is Binky."

Bernadette grimaced. Gloria laughed.

"Aw, don't look so glum sugar-plum." Gloria reached into her tight v-neck blouse and pulled out a slip of paper. "I got something for you. Was actually hoping you'd slide through tonight." She held out the folded white paper. Bernadette glanced up then around the bar.

"What's wrong? You always perk up for some strange." Gloria looked at her friend closely. "You don't look like you been sleepin' much. Little Iris been keeping you up?"

Bernadette cut her eyes and pursed her lips. She took a long gulp of beer. "Iris is just staying until she ready to go home. It's nothing."

"Well something got those bags under your eyes." Gloria searched her friend's face. "You been having that dream again?"

"Yeah," Bernadette said. "And it's worse. It's like I wake up from it, but I'm not really awake. It just keeps going. Like it's following me."

"Sounds like Type Two," Gloria said. "Waking up in a dream but you really dreaming. Some of the worse kinds of nightmares, baby. You want to talk about it?"

"Type Two, huh?" Bernadette sipped her beer. "You know you should have finished school."

"I got a degree in hard knocks, sweetness," Gloria said as she wiped at the bar. "I dole it out right here. My clients sit on stools instead of laying on couches." She winked.

Bernadette sighed and shook her head. Her eyes stinging with tears, she took a deep breath and forced a smile. Gloria handed her a napkin to wipe her eyes.

"You're coming apart, baby." Gloria said. The statement a matter of fact. "Iris is bringing it all down. I know you trying to help, sister-girl, but you're fragile yourself."

"How do you get through it, Gloria?" Bernadette gripped her beer.

Gloria looked away. "I don't think about it." She reached beneath the bar for the Johnny Walker. She poured two more shots. "I make myself forget. Sometimes with a little help." She slid the shot toward Bernadette. "A little of this, a little of that. You know Dr. Gloria has ways of getting what she needs to ease the pain."

Bernadette sighed. She eyed the shot before grabbing it. She turned the small, thick glass between her index finger and thumb. "This won't fix it, nor anything else 'Dr. Gloria' can get her hands on."

"What about this?" Gloria lifted the small folded paper she had pulled from her bra.

"Offering me a distraction?" Bernadette eyed the paper suspiciously. "A new woman, a new outlook on life?"

"If you want it." Gloria fanned the paper back and forth. "Do you want it?" she said. She waved the paper back and forth then poked it forward and pulled it back, trying to return the mood to light and lusty.

"I'm actually going to pass this time, Miss Gloria," Bernadette said, surprising herself.

"She's cute. Redbone. Slim and curvy. A dream to challenge them night-mares."

"Or a cheap thrill to add to my horrors. I need something else. Some-thing... I don't know."

"This might be it," Gloria said, raising her eyebrows up and down. "That something you're looking for."

"Love?" Bernadette said. "Piece of mind? Home?"

"Oh, shit. Miss Bernadette getting deep on us! Love? I don't know about that, sugar. You'd have to take that chance."

Bernadette shook her head.

Gloria tucked the paper back in her bra and poured another pair of shots. "You blowing my mind tonight, baby."

Bernadette crept back into her apartment after 2 a.m. Drunk but restless, she peeked in on Iris, who had been staying with her for a few days after fighting with her husband, Arthur.

"What you doing awake?" Bernadette asked.

"Can't sleep," Iris said. She was sitting up in bed flipping through a *Jet* Magazine. "Thinking about my babies. Wondering if they thinking about me. Trying to read this article about how Aretha bounced back. Maybe I can learn something." She smiled. The swelling had gone down, but a blue-black bruise marked the flesh underneath her eye and extended to the bridge of her nose. Just looking at Iris made Bernadette's heart ache.

Bernadette nodded. "Well, I was just checking in on you."

"Where were you? I mean, where do you go when you leave so late?"

Bernadette smiled her crooked smile, the right side of her wide mouth always rising higher than the left. It gave her face a vulnerable look, which she needed with eyes as intense and hard as hers. Bernadette's eyes looked black set against the shiny brass of her skin. She looked younger than her forty years, the eight years she had on Iris only registered when she spoke.

"Just out, you know. I have a good friend at Jimmy Cat's. She lets me come in after hours. Treats me right."

"Jimmy Cat's. I know that place. A little rough I've heard."

"Where'd you hear that?"

"Arthur. He stopped in there a time or two I guess."

"It's just a bar. Strong drinks and good music. I know the bartender there and a few of the dancers."

"You know I ain't one to judge," Iris said.

Bernadette blushed a little. "Just a place for drinks. A place to relax and take the edge off." She shrugged.

"Hell, if that's the case then I sorta wish Arthur went there more often. Have a drink after work and relax instead of coming home messing with me." Iris twisted her lips. The cut in her bottom lip, still red and puffy, looked painful to the touch.

"You ready to talk about it?" Bernadette asked. She walked into the room and sat down, her body causing a slight squeak of the bed.

Iris closed the magazine and placed it on her lap. Bernadette could already see the tears forming in her friend's eyes, and instantly, she felt sober. She rested her hand atop Iris's. "Tell me what happened."

Iris leaned her head against the wide mahogany headboard and closed her eyes. "Arthur don't really like it when I have people over to the house. But what the hell am I supposed to do at home with them kids all day? I get bored."

"I told you I can get your place back at The Avenue any time you want," Bernadette said. She missed Iris at work. The job, cleaning office buildings and hotel lobbies, more demoralizing than difficult, went easier when Iris cleaned alongside her, made things move faster, feel lighter.

"I know, I know." Iris wiped at her eyes. "And I'm thinking about it. I am. Anyway, I had sent the boys out and invited a few people over. We had some drinks, played some records, and..."

"When you say 'people,' what do you mean?" Bernadette asked.

"Oh, some fellas from around the way. Scratch, Terry, and three of their friends."

"Iris, you were entertaining five men while your kids were out playing and your husband was at work?"

"We was just drinking and listening to records. I grew up with Scratch and Terry and their friends were cool, so we was just catching up," Iris said. She flipped her hand dismissively. "So, Arthur came in and stood in the middle of the dining room yelling my name. Scratch and Terry and me was in the kitchen and the music was kinda loud so I didn't hear him." She shifted a little, touching the back of her neck nervously.

"Scratch turned off the record player. Then, I heard him, screaming my name like I was stuck on a mountain top somewhere. The way he looked at me when I came through the kitchen door, shit, I wished I *was* on a mountain top somewhere."

Bernadette frowned.

"Arthur yelled at everybody to get the hell outta his house. They split, too, swiped up the records and beer just as fast. I laughed at them. It was funny. They ran like the house was on fire. Arthur didn't like me laughing because he dropped his lunch box, stomped over to me, and grabbed me by the shoulders. Well, you know me, Bernadette, I pushed him. Next thing I know we having a shoving match. He pushed me hard enough to knock me through the doorway to the kitchen, and I fell into one of the kitchen chairs."

"Did he say anything?" Bernadette asked.

"Yeah. He was yelling. Respect this and sick and tired of that. I jumped up and yelled back. I told him to leave me alone and that I wasn't in the mood for his foolishness."

The bed squeaked as Bernadette brought a leg up and rested her elbow on her bended knee, leaning in, unblinking.

"Arthur stood there breathing all hard and shit. I moved to the stove and turned the skillet that I use to fry my chops down low. I was mad too, saying stuff too. 'I don't know who the hell you think you are busting in like you King Kong, running my company off,' I said. He said, 'I don't like all them people in my house.' I looked at him dead in his face. I said, 'I don't know what you worried about. If I was fooling around on you it wouldn't be in this house knowing you was coming home, shit, I'm a lot smarter than that, Arthur. You might be a fool but I'm not.' And that's when he slapped me across the face. 'I ain't nobody's fool,' he said. I cut my eyes at him, turned around, and said, 'Don't act like one then.' He grabbed me talking about I bet not ever call him a fool and I bet not ever turn my back to him. He slapped me again, and I grabbed a cast iron skillet from the range and went upside his head before I even thought about it."

Bernadette gasped and put a hand to her chest. "You hit him with the skillet?"

"Sure did. It had grease in it, too. Some of it splashed on his ear because he yelled 'Bitch' and spun around holding the side of his head. I dropped the skillet. Kinda scared, you know? Arthur squared up, his eyes like a damn grizzly. I picked the skillet back up. He came at me again, and I hit him again. He stumbled. Then I swung a real hard one, like I was gonna kill him, really knock him the hell out, because I was tired, you know, tired of fighting with his ass. He ducked it though."

Bernadette put her hand on Iris's thigh. "Then what did he do?"

"He jumped at me. Kept coming at me. So, I swung again and again 'till I swung one more time, one more good time, the kind of swing I thought would knock Arthur's head clean off," Iris said, wiping at her eyes. Her tears came in streams, but a mad excitement danced in her eyes. "I missed. It's like he knew that swing would be the one. He ducked and popped up like Joe Frasier. Caught me right in the eye. One punch. Never been hit so hard in my whole life. I fell flat on my damn back."

Bernadette's eyes went black and shiny as oil. She blinked hard and slow, trying to will the tears to stay put. She didn't want to cry, was tired of tears.

Iris lowered her voice. "I started to get up, pushing myself up..." Her throat caught on itself, but she didn't clear it. The words came out raspy and weak, the re-telling fragile and old, a story from long ago, the past flaring up in the constant fire of now. Everything is always happening now.

Iris continued, "He stomped over to me and kicked me in the stomach. I coughed and fell back down. He said, 'Stay down, bitch. Don't get up until I fucking tell you to.' So I did. I pressed my face to the floor. It was cool and kinda comforting on my face anyway. I just stayed there. Stayed down."

Iris wrapped her fingers around Bernadette's hand and squeezed. Bernadette tried to squeeze Iris's hand back, but she felt weak. Every part of her trembled. Maybe Gloria was right. Trying to help Iris was too much for her, yet it had always been Bernadette's way – helping, saving, loving.

"Arthur stood over me, and I looked up at him," Iris said. "He waited for a second to see if I was gonna move. I didn't. I didn't move a muscle. But when he went to step over me, I used the last little bit of strength I had and shot my fist right up between his legs. He yelled out, grabbing his balls, and I rushed up and out the damn door."

Bernadette cleared her throat and looked away, rage and sorrow, memory and nightmares surging against her rib cage, her heart suddenly too large for her body.

"I'm sorry," Bernadette said, the two words sincere but weak.

"Me, too," Iris said. "I'm glad you were home. I didn't know where else to go."

"Where's the boys?"

"I sent them over to Julia's soon as they got home from school. They ain't see none of it, but they ain't stupid. They know they get sent to Julia's when me and Arthur are fighting."

Bernadette didn't even attempt to wipe her eyes. Tears dripped from her chin; they left spots on her corduroys. "What can I do for you?" she asked. She tried to tell Iris with her eyes that she would do anything she wanted.

"I think I just need to rest." Iris lay back on the bed. She closed her eyes.

Bernadette took a deep breath and frowned. Iris didn't move. She laid there, her face swollen but peaceful. Bernadette watched her for a moment before she rose from the bed slowly. Iris reached out to her, opening her eyes.

"Will you lay with me? Just lay with me?" Iris said.

Iris slid over, making room for Bernadette. Still in her clothes and smelling faintly of smoke and booze, Bernadette rested herself next to her friend, spooning her, sighing with her, and silently crying with her.

Look it's Bernard. Hey Bernard. Can we call you Bernie? Bernie. Bernie. Bernie, everybody know you funny. Funny Bernie. Bull-dagger Bernie. Bull-dyke Bernie. Ball-busting Bitch Bernie. Dyke-bitch-need-a-good-dick Bernie. Need-a-good-dick Bernie. You need a good dick Bernie? Huh, Bernie? You need a good dick? Here you go Bernie. Here's a good dick for you, Bernie. Ain't so funny now is it, Bernie?

"NO!" Bernadette screamed out in her sleep. She was sweating, gnashing her teeth and biting the insides of her jaws. Blood, salty and disarmingly sweet, filled her mouth and she gagged. Coughing, she ran trembling hands over her afro, her hair damp and matted on the sides. She pulled her hands away from her head and clumps of hair came out in her hands. She ran her hands through her hair again. More hair. Small tufts of tight curls and matted knots of black and gray. She jumped up and ran into the bathroom, hitting her knee on the coffee table on the side of the couch. Blood continued to fill her mouth, the taste like baking soda mixed in sugar water. Bernie heaved. She finally made it into the bathroom. It was stark white. Too bright. The overhead light fluorescent, otherworldly, so white it was almost blue, like lightning.

Bernadette looked at herself in the mirror. Dark circles under jaundiced eyes and blood crusted at the corners of her mouth. She lifted her hands to her cheeks, strands and balls of hair between her fingers, her nails split and broken off at varying lengths. Her crusty, peeling lips twisted into a scowl. Her teeth like jagged stones, gargoyle teeth that didn't belong to her. She screamed out and her tongue, black and forked, flew out of her mouth and slammed into the mirror, a starburst of cracks overtook the mirror, but it did not shatter. The cracks spread, reaching out like vines, alive somehow, across the mirror to the walls and ceiling. Black curling cracks snaking all around the room, everything fracturing and breaking apart. The bathroom began to crumble and shake, flecks of white tile, chips of porcelain, and shards of glass floated around her like a snow globe, slicing and poking at her skin.

"Bernadette, Bernadette!" Iris shook her friend harder and harder. "Bernadette!"

Bernadette's arms flew forward and caught Iris in her still healing eye, knocking her out of the bed. Bernadette sat up with a start. She clutched her soaking wet shirt, the wide collar nearly dripping with sweat. She checked her face, teeth, and hair. Iris struggled to her feet, her hand cupped over her swollen eye.

"Damn, Bernie!" Iris said.

"Don't call me that." Bernadette said, panting. Cold sweat dripped between her breasts, and she shivered.

"What?" Iris said. She pushed at the dark blue flesh around the corner of her eye and winced.

"Bernie," Bernadette answered. The word bile in the back of her throat. She wiped her forehead with the back of her hand. "Don't call me 'Bernie.' Told you that before. I hate it."

"I'm sorry. I'm sorry. You just—" Iris sat down. She twisted and tugged at the lace that lined the double-stitched hem of the slip she wore as a night-gown. "I was... I was trying to wake you up. You were screaming."

"I'm sorry I hit you." Bernadette said. She looked around the room, still trying to orient herself. She glanced at Iris.

"It's all right." Iris looked at Bernadette. She put her hand on her friend's thigh. "Can I get you something? Do you need anything? You were so—you want some water or—"

"I'm fine." Bernadette hadn't meant for her voice to be so sharp, and she saw Iris stiffen out the corner of her eye. She pushed herself out of bed. She walked toward the bedroom door.

"Are you sure you're all right? Do you want to talk about it? It must have been a terrible dream because you—"

"Just go back to sleep, Iris." Bernadette disappeared into the darkness of the hall. In the bathroom, she stood in front of the mirror. Her face hidden in shadows, she refused to turn on the light. She touched her mouth, fingertips running over her lips and teeth. Afraid to look at herself, she leaned against the sink and cried.

When Bernadette returned to the bedroom, Iris was spreading the blankets across the bed. She wore one of Bernadette's shirts. It was too big, the arms folded up and pushed past her elbows.

"What's going on?" Bernadette asked.

"I'm going home," Iris said.

"It's five in the morning."

"I know." Iris grabbed her clothes. She folded them quickly and held them close to her chest. "I should go home. It's... it's time. I'm going to get my boys and..."

"What? Why? Why now?" Bernadette said. She leaned against the door jam.

"I was just thinking. Me and Arthur's fight. It was... serious. I almost killed him, Bernadette. I almost killed my children's father."

"Yeah, but he could kill you! The fighting. I know it's not the first time. So what about next time? There will be a next time. And a next time. And a next time!" Bernadette yelled, her voice straining. "Then there will be a last time, Iris. A. Last. Time." Her mouth hurt, her head and heart too.

Iris shook her head. "You don't understand. I've got to go home. I can't keep running away."

"Let's talk about it," Bernadette said. She hoped she didn't sound as desperate as she felt.

Iris walked up to Bernadette. She touched her face. Slowly, she leaned forward and kissed Bernadette's lips. The kiss, a careful press of lips, was sisterly, maternal even.

"Thank you, Bernadette." Iris smiled. "I appreciate you. I love you." She kissed her again, lighter and quicker, the touch over before it registered. Bernadette blinked, and it was over.

Past and present wrestled in Bernadette's chest as she tried to hush the noise in her head. She heard everyone's voices but her own. *I was tired, you know? So tired of fighting. Bull-dagger Bernie. Stay down.* She blinked then started to say something, but Iris pressed her fingers against Bernadette's lips.

"I know it's crazy, but I love him," Iris said. She tapped her finger against Bernadette's lips and sighed. She dropped her hand to her side.

"It is crazy. You're crazy," Bernadette said. She shook her head. The voices still there. The calm of the kiss still warming her skin, but fading, the comfort of it fading. "Shit. We all crazy." Bernadette moved aside. Iris slid past her.

Bernadette followed Iris into the hall, but Iris was moving so quickly she had already reached the door.

"Iris," Bernadette called out, uncertain of what she wanted to do or say.

Iris turned, her hand on the knob. "Crazy or not, I'm going to be fine. And you are, too."

"How do you know?" Bernadette asked.

"It's a woman thing, Bernie," Iris said. "We always fine even when we ain't."

"You believe that?"

Iris shrugged. She blew Bernadette a kiss and closed the door behind her.

Bernadette rang Gloria's doorbell tentatively. The sun was breaking the horizon, and the air was crisp but full with the smells of spring: flowers, dirt, and rain.

Gloria peeked through the sheer curtain on her door then opened the door quickly.

"Bernadette? Get your ass in here. What are you doing? What's wrong?" Gloria yanked her friend into the house. "Do you know what time it is?"

Bernadette nodded. Gloria ushered her to sit on the loveseat. "You look like shit. What happened? Is it Iris? Did Arthur come up to your place? Talk to me!"

"No. She left," Bernadette said. She tried to picture herself. She tried to see what Gloria saw. She knew her eyes were red and her hair was flat and uneven. She knew her clothes were wrinkled and funky from sweat and smoke, beer and whiskey.

"I don't know why she keeps going back to him," Bernadette said. She trembled and bit her lip against the truth. She certainly hadn't wanted Iris to go back to Arthur, but the anguish she felt had to do with a realization that came to her after Iris had closed the door. She was going back to her husband, her abusive, mean-spirited husband, and in her return to him, Iris was leaving Bernadette.

"I'm always thinking about it, Gloria," Bernadette said. "I can't get it out of my brain. All this time."

Gloria moved closer to Bernadette and put her arms around her. Bernadette let Gloria hold her. "I try to help people, try to save them, but it's me. I need help. I need saving," she said.

"Hush, baby, hush." Gloria rocked Bernadette in her arms, kissing the top of her head. She rocked her gently from side to side, rubbing her back and kissing her through the tight curls of her afro. Bernadette sobbed into her neck, her body shaking it. Gloria held her tight, still rocking and rubbing.

"Just you hush now. Relax, baby. Just relax," Gloria said. "Let me make you some tea or a hot toddy. That's what we need, warm brandy with a little honey. Don't that sound nice?" She kissed Bernadette's head once more and slowly released her. She held Bernadette's hands and looked into her eyes.

"I'm sorry," Bernadette mumbled. She sighed.

Gloria shook her head. "You ain't got nothing to be sorry about. Now, just wipe your face. Calm down. I'll make you something nice. Something to help." She stood up and walked swiftly to the kitchen.

Bernadette rested her head in her hands. Her thoughts all too ready to betray her, it all came flooding back, waves of rage and pain and dread, a tsunami of memory, destruction and despair washing over her.

They had been teenagers when it happened, she and Gloria, and they always looked out for one another. That night, Gloria had thrown rocks up at Bernadette's window to wake her, and when Bernadette came downstairs, she found her friend a bloody, disheveled mess. Her sweater torn, her bra missing, and her skirt twisted, Gloria shook uncontrollably, unable or unwilling to speak. She didn't have to speak. Bernadette knew what had happened by the look of her. She knew all too well the way Freddie and his boys pinched at titties and slapped at asses like it was some kind of game, the "Girl, we just playin' wit' your ole siddity ass!" never too far behind. Looking at the dried tear streaks on Gloria's cheeks and the chatter of her teeth, she knew her friend had fought when the game changed to a battle.

Bernadette snuck Gloria into the basement of her house and washed her up before setting up her father's old fold-away cot for her by the furnace. Bernadette sat with Gloria until she slept, then Bernadette took to the night dressed in her father's old work-shirt, 'Bernard' stitched across her left breast.

Crowbar in hand, she ran through alley after alley after alley, a fire burning in her chest. The cold cement numbed her feet inside her sneakers. Bernadette came up on Freddie's garage, the pale yellow paint chipped and cracked, the door pulled halfway down, a wide beam of light shining from underneath and smoke curling into the crisp October air. Feet shuffled when she lifted the garage door. Freddie and three other boys, all tall and bony except for one who was short and wide like a barrel grill, stood facing her. They laughed when they saw her. Laughed and began taunting her. They called her names, swiveling their hips, grabbing their crotches, and flicking their tongues at her.

"Bernard! It's Bernard! Bernie! BERNIE! Bernie. Bull-dagger Bernie. Ball-busting-need-a-dick-Bernie. You need a good dick, Bernie?"

Freddie had stepped forward, spitting then licking his lips at Bernadette. 'I got a good dick,' he had said. He moved to grab her. Bernadette swung the crowbar. He ducked. She swung again. He moved aside. She swung again, her hardest swing yet, and Freddie dipped low. On the way up, he caught her in the stomach with an uppercut, and she doubled over dropping her weapon. He pulled his fist way back and punched Bernadette, one quick, hard, calculated punch that knocked her down. He spit on her and said, "You stay down."

The rest is a blur, a blur of sour spit and sharp teeth, ripping flesh and dirty nails, trembling muscles and pressing, pressing, pressing against an oily, gritty garage floor. She felt herself cracking, every part of her shattering under the weight of their sweat-funky bodies. They broke her, her mind, heart, everything, fragmented and cracked and broken beyond repair.

Gloria startled her with a tap on the shoulder. She jumped then blinked back tears. She swallowed hard to catch her breath.

"I'm sorry," Gloria said. She put a hand on Bernadette's shoulder. "Here you go, sugar." She gave her a steaming mug and waited for Bernadette to sip from it. Bernadette just stared at the steam as it curled from the cup then evaporated into nothing.

"Go 'head," Gloria said. "It'll calm you. I promise. Then, when you're all relaxed, you can lie back and tell me everything. The doctor is in, baby."

Bernadette looked at Gloria, who nodded assuredly with a small, forced smile. Bernadette took one sip. A small one. She held the hot liquor and honey in her mouth and swallowed slowly. It slid down her throat sweet and easy. Her face tingled with warmth.

"Good, right?" Gloria said. "Drink some more."

Bernadette took a deep breath, inhaling the vapors from the cup. She looked up at Gloria, dropped her eyes, then looked past her. On the television across from where she sat, Bernadette saw a small piece of folded paper. It sat atop the television set like a tent, or the roof of a tiny house, a home. Bernadette wanted to go home but wondered if her apartment qualified. It was cold there. It was lonely there. It was sad there.

"Take another sip," Gloria said, sternly.

"I need more honey," Bernadette said. "You know I like it sweet." She forced a wink and crooked grin. Home. Home sweet home. She looked at the folded paper, the roof to her tiny home. Maybe. Maybe it could be just that. She cleared her throat.

"And fix you one, too," Bernadette said. "Probably just what we both need."

Gloria stood and smiled. "You got it, sistergirl. I'll fix me one up and bring some more sweet for the sweet." She winked then moved past Bernadette to head into the kitchen.

While Gloria was in the kitchen, Bernadette crept across the room and snatched the folded paper off the television. She read the name to herself then read it again, saying the name aloud, "Ruby Red." She read the phone number silently.

She smiled despite herself and tucked the number into the front pocket of her corduroys. She left her cup where the number had been, smoothed down the front of her shirt, then snuck out the front door.

Special Thanks

This book, in both its original and anniversary editions, represents love and encouragement, inspiration and support, across so many communities and relationships. I want to thank the following people and organizations:

I would like to thank my mama, Pamela Wilson, my pops, Wilbert Wilson, my sisters Peaches and Tiffany, and my nieces and nephews. My family's support of my writing dream is a large part of how it became a reality. Thank you to my wife, Jasmine Smith. You are my home. Always. Thank you to my oldest and dearest friends, who serve as sounding boards and trusted readers, bullshit detectors and cheerleading squads: Khaulah Naima Nuruddin (I couldn't put this book out without your careful editing and honest feedback), Adella Deacon, and Tassany Prasoeuthsy. Thank you to my Tampa writing community who keep me inspired and engaged: Slam Anderson, Adrien Julious-Butler, Silk-Jazmyne Hindus, Jasmin Lankford, Dennis Amadeus, Walter "Wally B." Jennings, Gloria Munoz, LeQuina Knox, Tiffany Razzano, Immani Love Brown, Andrea Assaf, and Lorin Oberweger. Thank you to my broader, and just as essential writing community, from places both near and far, but most especially: Dara Mathis, Alexa Bryant, and Eesha Pandit. Tremendous gratitude to Fiona Zedde, whose guidance and support made this book possible over a decade ago and continues to encourage the realization of my writing career in all of its shapes and forms. Thank you to Christina Arenas, Ashley Butler, and Nikotris Perkins, my Ain't No Extra Credit crew. Thank you Chastity Pascoe and Seed for the dope cover design. Thank you to the Oral Fixation community (throwback), Kitchen Table Literary Arts, Charis Books and More, Women and Children's First, Wordier Than Thou, Heard 'Em Say, The Poets at USF, The Porch, Story Studio Chicago, Free Expressions, 2nd Story, Bluestockings Collective, VONA, Yaddo, the Ragdale Foundation, Astraea Lesbian Justice Fund, Giovanni's Room, Black Lesbian Fiction Press, Renee Bess, Trelani "So Fundamental" Michelle, Kat Williams, Rena Reads, Lauren Cherelle, Dr. Stephanie Andrea Allen, Amtul Nuruddin, Dr. Carleah East, Donald Gordon, Asa Gordon, Patty McNair, Christine Rice, Dan Prazer, April Newman, Shaquea Moore, Nelka Barnes, James Lower, Ilana Shabanov, Tony Bowers, Jessica Young Chang, Angela Gabriel, Megan Stielstra, Eric May, Iya Ifatola Adesanya, Jason Martinez, and Sara Slawnik. Thank you, thank you, thank you to my Patreon Community, whose support for me and my work is outta this world!

If I've missed your name in these acknowledgements, please know that so many of you are in my heart and an essential part of this journey even if not listed in this frenzied, climbing-through-the-years list of folks who made this book possible. I love you. All of you.

About the Author

Sheree L. Greer is a writer, artist, teacher, and publisher living in Tampa, Florida. In 2014, she founded The Kitchen Table Literary Arts Center to showcase and support the work of Black women and women of color writers and is the author of two novels, *Let the Lover Be* and *A Return to Arms*, a short story collection, *Once and Future Lovers,* and the student writing guides, *Stop Writing Wack Essays* and *Baddest Out of Your Friends.* Her work has been published in *First Bloom Anthology, LezTalk Anthology, VerySmartBrothas, Autostraddle, The Windy City Times, Bleed Literary Journal, Rumpus Magazine,* the *Windy City Queer Anthology: Dispatches from the Third Coast,* and more. Sheree has received a Union League of Chicago Civic Arts Foundation award, earned her MFA at Columbia College Chicago, and is a VONA/VOICES alum, Astraea Lesbian Foundation for Justice grantee, Yaddo fellow, and Ragdale Artist House Rubin Fellow. Her essay, "Bars" published in *Fourth Genre Magazine,* was nominated for a Pushcart Prize and notably named in *Best American Essays 2019.* Her latest essays, "None of this is Bullshit" and "101 Reasons/Tell the Truth" can be found online.

More about the author at www.shereelgreer.com

Additional Titles by Sheree L. Greer

Fiction

Let the Lover Be

A Return to Arms

Nonfiction

Stop Writing Wack Essays: a Student Writing Guide

Baddest Out of Your Friends: Grammar and Usage Basics

www.ingramcontent.com/pod-product-compliance
Lightning Source LLC
Chambersburg PA
CBHW040910010826
48978CB00013BB/1220